Dictionary Plus *for* WOMEN

An information guide book regarding:

Hysterectomies, Menopause, & Related Topics

By

Suzette Buhr, R.T.R.

First Edition

© 2002, 2003 by Suzette Buhr R.T.R. All rights reserved.

No part of this book may be reproduced, stored in a retrieval system, or transmitted by any means, electronic, mechanical, photocopying, recording, or otherwise, without written permission from the author.

ISBN: 1-4033-9442-3 (e-book)
ISBN: 1-4033-9443-1 (Paperback)
ISBN: 1-4033-9584-5 (Hardcover)

Library of Congress Control Number: 2003090130

This book is printed on acid free paper.

Printed in the United States of America
Bloomington, IN

To order additional copies of Dictionary Plus for Women,
visit on-line at:
www.dictionaryplusforwomen.com
or contact 1stBooks Library direct at:
www.1stbooks.com

1stBooks – rev. 02/10/03

Acknowledgements

To my editor and personal physician: Dr. Robert Christmann, M.D. OB/GYN, I thank you very much for all your medical expertise and knowledge. I am forever grateful for all the dedicated years of service that you have provided for me, for my numerous female medical needs, and for graciously taking the time to edit the medical portion of this *Dictionary Plus for Women*.

To my assistant editor and daughter: Alicia Buhr, I thank you from the bottom of my heart for critiquing and editing several of my rough drafts. I am so very blessed by your kindness and patience.

To Nature Made Nutritional Products: I thank you for your prompt responses and information provided by your on-line team of Wellness Advisors.

To Wendy Stewart, Sheila Lewis, Londa Boots, Michelle Hubbard and everyone at 1st Books Library: I thank you all for helping to make this publication possible.

I would also like to express special thanks to Barbara Fell, Libbie Kacuba, Linda Knapton-Brumm, Lisa Petersen, Jenny Redmann, Machell Scott, and my many friends and co-workers for sharing their thoughts, feelings, and personal experiences with me.

Dedication

I dedicate this book to all women:
past, present, and future generations,
and
in loving memory of
my Grandma Lucille Jones.

Important Notice & Disclaimer

IMPORTANT NOTICE: This information guide book is intended to assist women with a better understanding of potential medical conditions. This is a reference volume only, *not* a medical manual. It is *not* intended to diagnose any particular symptom or disease. The information given here is designed to help women make informed decisions about their health. When it comes to patient choices and decisions regarding treatment and diagnosis, you must discuss those with your physician. This book is *not* intended as a substitute for any medical treatment that your physician prescribes or prescribed. If you suspect that you have a medical problem, we urge you to see your health care professional.

DISCLAIMER: Please be aware that medical information, medical procedures, medical advancements, medical terminology, and medicine itself is constantly changing, therefore it is important that you check with your health care professional regarding any questions you may have. The author of this book is *not* a medical physician and does *not* claim to diagnose any conditions or disease. Portions of this book are unedited.

Contents

Acknowledgements iii
Dedication v
Important Notice & Disclaimer vii
History: Timeline 1
Women's Dictionary 9
Medical Terminology Made Simple 69
Anatomical Illustrations 71
HRT / ERT Information 75
Herbal Dictionary 79
Vitamin Dictionary 89
Mineral Dictionary 97
Facts 105
Marketing & Manufacturing 111
Advice 115
Important Resources 117
Bibliography 125
About the Author 135
More Dictionary Plus Titles 137

History: Timeline

60,000 years ago... evidence of herbal remedies found in the burial sites of Neanderthal man, uncovered in 1960, in a cave in northern Iraq.

2800 years ago... first written record of use of herbal remedies, used in China.

4000 years ago... soybeans were cultivated in Northern China and Inner Mongolia.

3000 years ago... soybeans spread through out Asia, Japan, and Korea.

1800's... soybeans arrive in the United States from China and Europe.

1887... the National Institute of Health was born. It began in a one-room laboratory in New York, for the research on cholera and other infectious diseases. Since then, it has grown into 27 different institutes, centers, and organizations. The NIH researches and reports results to the public on a variety of topics. (Most current information, noted in this Timeline, during July, 2002.)

* For a listing of the 27 NIH Institutes and Centers, go on-line at: http://www.nih.gov/icd/

1890's... scientific investigations began regarding the menstrual cycle.

1900's... during the early 1900's, medicinal herbs began being used extensively, due to the short supply of pharmaceutical drugs available, during World War I.

1920's... the post war period creates a renewed expansion within the pharmaceutical industries. (Although a small number of herbalists, keep the tradition of herbal medicine alive.)

1920's... soybeans became used in the U.S. for their oils.

1926... looking for the "Fountain of Youth", begins.

1930's... soybeans became used in the U.S. for animal feed.

1930's... Dr. John Harvey Kellogg developed the use of soybeans in cereals and granolas for human consumption.

1937... hormones were being used, experimentally, to help women cope with hot flashes and menopausal symptoms.

1937... the National Institute of Cancer became established. This institute leads the effort to reduce the burden of cancer morbidity and mortality. The goal is to stimulate support and scientific discovery, to provide research and training, and to conduct and support programs that aid in prevention, detection, diagnosis, treatment, and cure.

1930's-1940's... hormone injections were manufactured and used by German scientists and doctors for their female patients.

1942... Ayerst Laboratory introduces Premarin estrogen tablets. The world's 1st conjugated estrogen product in the United States and Canada.

1940's... women and their doctors claim that estrogen is the "cure all" for youth, sexuality and longevity.

1946... the World Health Organization became established. Their mission: to attain the highest possible level of health, for all people, including physical, mental, and social well-being, not merely the absence of disease or infirmity.

1962... the National Institute of Child Health and Human Development became established. The NICHHD provides research into the areas of fertility/infertility, pregnancy, growth & development, and medical rehabilitation.

1960's... during the mid 1960's, the news and press published many articles promoting Estrogen Replacement Therapy, stating estrogen keeps women looking and feeling youthful.

1968... the British Herbal Medicine Association is founded.

1970's... it became obvious that post menopausal women taking estrogen alone had an increased risk of endometrial cancer.

1970's... during the early 1970's, scientists noted the toxic effects of xenoestrogens within our environment could cause serious health problems, including cancers, and reproductive defects that may be passed to future generations.

1970's... during the mid 1970's, Mayo Clinic consensus conference concluded that estrogen should never be given to any woman with a uterus in tact (any woman who has *not* had a hysterectomy).

1974... the National Institute of Aging was established.

1974... the idea of a National Women's Health Network was conceived by two women who envisioned the day when the women's health movement would have full fledged lobby in Washington, D.C. By 1976, the Board met in Washington to draw up by-laws to build a

Dictionary Plus for WOMEN

strong women's health advocacy presence in the nation's capital. Their mission is to advocate for national policies that protect and promote all women's health and provide evidence-based independent information to empower women to make fully informed health decisions. Since they act as an independent voice for women's health, they accept no money from companies that sell pharmaceuticals, medical devices, dietary supplements, alcohol, tobacco, or health insurance. They research and analyze women's health issues, free from the influence of corporate interests.

1970's... by the late 1970's, evidence was mounting that caused concern linking estrogen to increased risk of breast cancer.

1979... DES (Diethylstilbestrol: a synthetic estrogen that was taken by approximately four million women, in the U.S. and Europe, between 1948 and 1971 to prevent miscarriage, to treat breast cancer, and to reduce menopausal symptoms), was banned in 1979 due to the mounting evidence that related a high incidence of cervical cancers found in young women, was traced back to their mothers, who were prescribed DES during their pregnancy to prevent miscarriage. Further research showed that the use of DES in pregnancy is also linked to infertility, other cancers, and birth defects in the children who do survive. (DES was also used for livestock feed to fatten them up for market, until it was banned in 1979.)

1980's... during the early 1980's, studies showed that by adding progesterone to estrogen decreased the risk of certain cancers in women.

1980's... the era of massive research, studies and investigations. Conflicting reports, depending upon what clinic/hospital, pharmaceutical company, or organization fronts the study. Who to believe?, Who to trust?, What to do?, Where to turn?, Huge decisions for women to make regarding their own medical care.

1984... funding for Alzheimer's Disease centers by the National Institute of Aging began, providing research for prevention and cures.

1986... the National Institute of Arthritis and Musculoskeletal and Skin Diseases became established. This area supports the research into the causes, treatment and prevention of arthritis, muscular, skeletal, and skin diseases.

1990's... women's health clinics that create and sell individually mixed hormone prescriptions, pop-up in the United States.

1990's... soybeans become popular in the United States. Many articles, and scientific research proving the benefits of soy.

1994... xenoestrogen controversy arrives in congress, letting corporate America decide which they prefer: petrochemical use for their products (and increased profits) that may cause increased xenoestrogens in the environment / or / drastic changes in production (costing millions of dollars and uncertainty if the current population accepts the changes) that will benefit the health of human society.

1994... study showed that small doses of progesterone given to menopausal women, restored their sex drive.

1995... a study, the PEPI (Postmenopausal Estrogen/Progestin Intervention) trial, examined effects of sex hormones on cholesterol and the endometrium. This trial found that estrogen taken alone "significantly increased the occurrence of severe hyperplasia in women who had *not* had a hysterectomy." (Hyperplasia is considered to be a step along the pathway to cancer.) This study also showed that estrogen did lower total cholesterol and raise HDL (good cholesterol).

July 9, 2002... The National Institute of Health's National Heart, Lung, and Blood Institute announced to the public: that they had stopped early (3 years early) a major clinical trial, by the Women's Health Initiative, studying the effects of commonly used form of estrogen plus progestin. This study of more than 16,000 healthy menopausal women followed for an average of 5.2 years, found strong evidence for significantly increased risk of invasive breast cancer, cardiovascular disease, stroke, and blood clots. Researchers found that the combination hormone medication used in clinical trials posed more risks than benefits.

Study Statistics:

22%	increase risk of cardiovascular disease
29%	increase risk of heart attacks
26%	increase risk of breast cancer
100%	increase risk of blood clots
38%	increase risk of stroke
—%	increase risk of gall bladder disease (—exact % unknown)
37%	decrease reduction of colorectal cancer
33%	decrease reduction of hip fractures

* For more information, go on-line to: http://www.whi.org
* For more information about hormone replacement therapy call the National Cancer Institute at: 1-800-422-6237

For the hearing impared, call the NCI at: 1-800-332-8615

July 16, 2002... The National Cancer Institute released the results of a study regarding: ovarian cancer risks for women taking estrogen only. This study followed 44,000 women for 20 years, finding that the women who used estrogen-only therapy for prolonged use were 60% more likely to develop ovarian cancer than women who did not use hormone replacement therapy. This study is consistent with the findings of two other recent reports.

* This report by the National Cancer Institute was published in the July 17, 2002 issue of JAMA.
* For more information about this study, go on-line to: http://www.nih.gov
* For a variety of hormone information, go on-line to: www.cancer.gov
* For more information about hormone replacement therapy call The National Cancer Institute at: 1-800-422-6237

For the hearing impared, call the NCI at: 1-800-332-8615

July 2002... JAMA (Journal of the American Medical Association) published a study by the Palo Alto Medical Foundation. The study of the "Risks and Benefits of Estrogen Plus Progestin in Healthy Postmenopausal Women" demonstrated that the clinical outcomes were basically the same as their previous studies and similar to the findings of studies performed by organizations associated with the National Institute of Health, during the year 2002. The PAMF stated they stopped their study early due to the number of excessive breast cancers exceeded the warning threshold, and the overall risks exceeded the benefits of the hormone use. (See the History: Timeline, Study Statistics of July 9, 2002 Women's Health Institute information.)

August 21, 2002... JAMA (Journal of the American Medical Association) released the results of a study that evaluated Ginko supplements and its short term effects on memory, learning, attention, and concentration. The data collected during this six week study suggested: that when taking Ginko and following the manufacturers instructions, it provided no measurable benefit in memory or related cognitive function to adults with healthy cognitive functions. (However, further studies are set to conclude in 2006 in regards to Ginko possibly preventing dementia.)

Dictionary Plus for WOMEN

Women's Dictionary

Word:	**Abdominopelvic Region**
Definition:	The part of the body that is located between the chest and pelvis. The peritoneum lines this cavity. The organs in this region include: stomach, small and large intestines, liver, gall bladder, spleen, pancreas, bladder, ovaries, fallopian tubes, and uterus.
Condition:	Peritonitis is an inflammation of the membranous lining in the abdominopelvic cavity. This may be caused by an infectious organism that gains access into the internal organs by any of the following ways: female genital tract, operative incision, piercing the abdominal wall, perforated ulcer, ruptured appendix, blood stream, or lymphatic vessels.
Treatment:	Depending on the nature of the condition, or disease, an antibiotic therapy may be necessary or possibly surgical intervention.
Word:	**Adhesion**
Definition:	The abnormal union of adjacent bodily tissues.
Condition:	Often times, after an abdominal surgery, adhesions form during the healing process. These adhesion often consist of blood and connective tissues. It is this form of scar tissue that binds the affected surfaces inside the

Treatment: abdomen. Pain and bleeding can occur as the adhesions pull apart from an organ or part within the body.
Exercise is effective in decreasing adhesions. If adhesions cause persistent pain or difficulty, they may be separated surgically during a laparoscopy.

Word: **Adrenal Glands**
Definition: A triangular shaped gland that covers the superior surface of each kidney. These glands secrete hormones that regulate metabolism and the chemical composition of body fluids. The adrenal gland has two parts. The inner portion is called the medulla. The medulla produces adrenaline (also known as epinephrine) and norepinephrine. The outer portion is called the cortex. The cortex produces the steroid hormones: cortisol (also know as hydrocortisone), aldosterone, and testosterone.
Condition: Possible conditions and diseases of the adrenal cortex may include:
1.) Addison's Disease: which causes hyposecretion of the adrenal cortex causing destruction of the adrenal gland by infection, or by an autoimmune attack.
2.) Cushing's Syndrome: which causes over production of cortisol.
3.) Cohn's Syndrome: which causes over production of aldosterone.
4.) Adrenal Cortex Tumors: which may cause over production of hormones.
5.) Adrenal Cancer: difficult to diagnose due to the wide variety of symptoms.
Treatment: Treatment varies depending on the diagnosis.

Word: **Alternative Medicine**
Definition: A type of treatment or therapy that promotes good physical health and a positive mental outlook. Alternative medicine may be used in addition to /or/ in place of traditional western medical treatment.

Condition: Alternative medicines may be used to help a person increase strength, decrease blood pressure, lower stress levels, increase immunity response, improve cardiovascular health, decrease PMS symptoms, decrease pain, and promote positive emotional well-being.

Treatment: These additional treatment options encompass the following styles for healing the body and mind: aromatherapy, acupuncture, accupressure, biofeedback, chiropractic, energy healing, guided imagery, herbal remedies, massage therapy, meditation, reflexology, Tai Chi, and Yoga. Most alternative medicines tend to focus on breathing, relaxation, posture, positive mental outlook, getting plenty of rest, developing healthy eating habits, avoiding alcohol, avoiding tobacco, avoiding other drugs, and using the body's natural energy to aid in the healing process. Alternative medicines usually incorporate self participation regarding the individuals own medical treatment. This allows the individual to draw from their own values, ideas, lifestyles, and spiritual beliefs that help to aid in their own healing process.

Word: **Anemia**

Definition: A condition in which there is a reduction of the number of red blood corpuscles or a reduction of the total amount of hemoglobin in the bloodstream.

Condition: Anemia can occur when a woman has heavy, long, or irregular periods. Hemorrhaging with fibroid tumors, endometriosis, or cancer can also cause anemia.

Treatment: Treatment for anemia is increasing ones Iron intake. Sources of Iron include: Ferrous Gluconate (Iron pills), Vitamins with Iron, and Slim Fast nutritional supplement. Vegetables high in Iron include: green or leafy vegetables such as spinach, broccoli, or peas. Fruits high in Iron include: apricots, prunes, and raisins. Meats and fish high in Iron include: oysters, clams, liver, fish, beef, pork, and lamb. Seeds high in

Dictionary Plus for WOMEN

Info:	Iron include: nuts, pumpkin seeds, and sunflower seeds. Cereals high in Iron include: Co-Co Wheats, Crispix, Cheerios, and Rice Chex. Sometimes Iron supplements, or digesting large amounts of food that are high in Iron, may cause constipation.
Word:	**Anesthesia (Anesthetic)**
Definition:	An agent that produces partial or total loss of sensation, with or without loss of consciousness. Anesthetics are used to inhibit normal body reflexes to make surgery safer and easier to perform.
Condition:	There are four types of anesthesia used. Each is dependent upon the body part that requires the surgery and the patient's needs. Local anesthetics are usually used for smaller areas that do *not* require the patient to be unconscious. Example: to remove a foreign object from the tip of a finger, or remove a small growth on the surface of the skin. Regional anesthetics, such as a spinal or an epidural, are sometimes given if a patient needs a large area numbed and also needs to be alert or conscious during the procedure. Example: frequently used during childbirth. Sedation, also known as twilight sleep, is a state of reduced consciousness where as strong stimuli, loud noises, or bright lights can awake the patient. Example: having dental work done. Nitrous Oxide (laughing gas) is an inhaled anesthetic, that is mixed with oxygen, that may be used in combination with other anesthetics. General anesthetics are often used when the patient needs to be unconscious and unaware of any pain during the procedure. Example: for abdominal and pelvic surgeries. Sodium Pentothal is often the medication used as a general anesthetic at the beginning of the surgery which allows the patient to drift off to sleep. General anesthetics can be administered in the form of a gas, volatile liquid, or injectable.

Treatment:	Anesthetics are used as a form of treating pain, producing a relaxed or unconscious state, blocking the memory of a procedure, and helping to make a surgery easier to perform by inhibiting the normal body reflexes. Side effects of anesthesia can include: constipation, nausea, vomiting, headache, blurred vision, nightmares, shivering or trembling, muscle pain, mood changes, or sore throat. * For more information about anesthetics, look on-line at: http://www.howstuffworks.com/anesthesial.htm http://www.findarticles.com
Word:	**Arthritis**
Definition:	Inflammation of a joint, usually accompanied by pain, swelling and a change in structure. There are two main types: Osteo Arthritis and Rheumatoid Arthritis.
Condition:	The two most common types of arthritis are osteo and rheumatoid. Osteo arthritis is: known as the disease of old age. It affects men as well as women who are usually over the age of 40. Osteo arthritis usually forms at the site of a previous injury or an area of overuse. It causes degeneration and inflammation of the cartilage in the joint. It also causes overgrowth of bone, spur formations, and impaired function. It is a chronic disease involving the joints, especially the weight bearing joints (hips and knees). Rheumatoid arthritis is: a chronic systemic disease (autoimmune condition). It tends to affect more females than males. The larger joints are usually affected first and usually bilateral (on both sides of the body). It is noted by inflammation of the synovial membrane which line the joints. These changes in the joints and related structures cause a constantly deteriorating condition that results in crippling deformities. Another condition that seems common for people with Rheumatoid arthritis to have is Sjogren's Syndrome (dry mouth). It is thought that both stem from autoimmune diseases.

	*For more information see the word "Mouth" on page 44.
Treatment:	Possible short term therapy may include anti-inflammatory medications such as Aspirin, Ibuprofen or corticosteroids. These medications do *not* cure the disease or prevent the progression of it, however, they may help the patient tolerate the pain and swelling associated with arthritis. Cold packs may also be recommended during certain times to reduce swelling and inflammation. According to an article published in the March 2000 Journal of the American Medical Association, glucosamine was shown to have positive effects for osteo arthritis sufferers by reducing the symptoms and stimulating growth of new cartilage while maintaining existing cartilage. Most rheumatologists would recommend keeping the joints active and flexible by using gentle, comfortable motions and avoid any strenuous, sharp, hard, or fast movements. For some severe cases of arthritis, surgery may be recommended. * For more information contact the National Arthritis Foundation at: 1-800-242-9945.
Word:	**Bio-identical Hormone (BHRT)**
Definition:	A hormone replacement therapy that may be made with any combination of yam, soy, progesterone, testosterone, DHEA (dehydroepiandrosterone), pregnenolone, estradiol, estrone, estriol, cortisol, melatonin, HGH (Human Growth Hormone), or Thyroid T3 & T4.
Info:	Bio-identical information is difficult to understand, due to the fact that many companies who sell hormone based products try to entice consumers with "appealing-type" words. These clever phrases or twist on words are then used to sell their products. The word Bio-identical hormone is also referred to as "natural" hormone. However, Bio-identical hormones are made in laboratories using pharmaceutical-grade chemicals.

Dictionary Plus for WOMEN

It is this chemical structure, *not* the actual source of where the hormone came from, that will determine if it can be called a Bio-identical hormone. Bio-identical hormones may be an identical chemical match to a particular hormone, however this does *not* mean that it will metabolize in the human body in the same way that a human hormone would. It is the human body's complex interactions and its ability to recognize its own hormones vs. identical chemical compounds that can sometimes create side effects or serious health risks.

Condition: When any of these hormone levels become depleted, or do *not* function properly, the quality and quantity of life may become compromised. Hormone difficulties can cause a wide variety of symptoms including: mood swings, weight gain, fibrocystic breasts, irregular periods, infertility, PMS, decreased sex drive, vaginal dryness, hot flashes, night sweats, depression, memory loss, sleep disorders, heart disease, and osteoporosis.

Treatment: A simple saliva test can determine a person's hormone levels. It is with this information that a specialty compounding pharmacy can than create a pill that is tailor made for each individual woman. It is these individualized hormone mixtures that are meant to provide each individualized woman a maximum relief of symptoms with minimal side effects. You must discuss and weigh the risks vs. benefits with your physician before taking a Bio-identical Hormone Replacement Therapy medication.

Word: **Biopsy**
Definition: The removal of a small piece of tissue, that will be further tested and examined for abnormal cells. "Conization" is a biopsy procedure that may be done if a larger, cone-shaped-wedge section needs to be removed for study and evaluation.

Condition: An abnormal Pap Test may have lead to the recommendation of the biopsy. During a biopsy,

	whenever possible, the entire affected area in question may be removed. Other times, it is only possible to remove a small sample of the tissue. A biopsy may detect a variety of normal and abnormal cellular changes.
Treatment:	It generally takes a couple of days for the laboratory to test the tissue and to send a final report to your physician. The results will determine a treatment plan that is right for you.
Word:	**Bladder Infection**
Definition:	An infection located in the bladder.
Condition:	Women are more prone to bladder infections due to the fact that the urethra is located near the vagina and anus, making it more easily contaminated from these sources. Those at greater risk of bladder infections are menopausal women, pregnant women, smokers, and those who use diaphragms. Some possible causes that may increase the likelihood of infections may include: frequent sexual activity especially when it is combined with vaginal dryness, hormonal imbalances, and / or taking hormone replacement therapy.
Treatment:	Most bladder infections are treated with antibiotics such as Macrobid or Sulfa. Other ways to lessen the chance of getting a bladder infection include: drinking plenty of water, urinate frequently, rinse and clean the genital area daily, do *not* use strong scented soaps or bubble baths, wear cotton underwear (*not* nylon), be careful with certain types of laundry detergent, use a vaginal lubricant before intercourse such as K-Y Gel, using vaginal applications of estrogen cream tend to work well at restoring hormone imbalances and decreasing the chance of future urinary tract infections, and do *not* use powder, talc, perfumes or feminine sprays on or around the genital areas.

Word: **Blood Clot**
Definition: Also known as Thrombus (Thrombosis) or Embolism. It is the process when blood thickens into a non-fluid like mass. This blood coagulation form is then called a clot.
Condition: Blood clots may be caused from a variety of situations including: uterine fibroids, endometriosis, post-surgical complications, heart disorders, obesity, menstrual difficulties, or the use of hormone replacement therapy. Blood clots can occur in many parts of the body. Most common being veins and arteries in the legs. Blood clots can block a vessel and stop the blood supply to an organ or part. Symptoms may range from local pain, tenderness, swelling, change of skin color, to sudden death.
Treatment: Depending on the location of the clots, the number of clots and the severity, treatment may include: warm water soaks, heating pad, special stockings for the patients legs, bed rest, or blood thinning (anticoagulant) medication such as aspirin therapy or Coumadin (also known as warfarin sodium). If severe clotting is caused from uterine fibroids or endometriosis, surgical intervention may be necessary.
* For more information on "Fibroid Tumor" see page 29.
* For more information on "Endometriosis" see page 23.

Word: **Bone Densitometry**
Definition: A radiology procedure that measures the amount of density in a person's bones.
Condition: This procedure may be recommended for women who have gone through menopause to help assess the amount of bone loss due to decreased estrogen levels.
Treatment: In preparation of the scan, it may be recommended to refrain from taking any calcium supplements the day prior to and the day of the scan, and to wear comfortable clothing without zippers, snaps, or

buttons. The procedure will begin with the patient lying on a x-ray table. It will use x-ray energy to scan a particular area of the body, an area that may be at risk of possible fractures, such as the hip or spine. A Rheumatologist or Endocrinologist may interpret the exam and informs the patient's primary physician of the results. It is this information that is used in determining how to help the patient reduce their risk of osteoporosis fractures.

Word:
Definition: **Breast Cancer and Breast Information**
The upper, front part of the chest, that provides the main function of producing milk for an infant after the birth of a child.

Condition: According to the American Cancer Society, if you notice any changes that occur in or around either of your breasts, you should see your health care professional as soon as possible for an evaluation. These changes may include: lumps, swelling, skin irritation or dimpling, nipple pain or retraction, redness or scaliness of the nipple or breast skin, or a discharge other than milk.

Treatment: There are a variety of exams that may be used to help diagnose a breast cancer, and those may include: mammography, ultrasound, breast biopsy, computerized tomography, and magnetic resonance imaging (MRI). The type of treatment recommended would depend upon the diagnosis. Treatments may include: lumpectomy, radical or partial mastectomy, radiation, and/or chemotherapy.

Early diagnosis is the most useful key for breast cancer survival.

The American Cancer Society recommends:
* Women ages 20 and over should perform monthly self breast exams.
* Women ages 20-39 should have a breast exam every 3 years.

*   Women ages 40 and above should have an annual breast exam and annual mammogram.
*   For current guidelines and information about breast screenings, breast self exams, mammograms, breast cancer, mammogram screening coverage laws in each state, the use of computer-aided technology, digital mammography, and the use of MRI for breast screening in high risk women, please contact the American Cancer Society at: 1-800-ACS-2345, or visit on-line at: www.cancer.org

Word: **Calcium**
*   See the word "Calcium" listed in the Mineral section on page 98.

Word: **Cancer**
Definition: All forms of cancer involve an abnormal growth and spread of malignant cells.
Condition: Cancers of the reproductive system (uterus, cervix, and ovaries) are often the most fatal of all cancers. When a cancer spreads within the body from one site to a new site, it is called metastasis.
Treatment: Early diagnosis is crutial. Routine Pap Tests, breast exams, and pelvic exams can help detect an early onset of cancer. Reporting any abnormal findings to your physician will also lead to a more prompt diagnosis. Some cancers of the reproductive system may require surgery plus radiation or chemotherapy.
*   For more information, contact the American Cancer Society at 1-800-ACS-2345, or visit on-line at: www.cancer.org

Word: **Cervix**
Definition: It is the constricted lower end of the uterus. This is the portion that joins the uterus to the vagina. It is approximately one inch in length.
Condition: Diseases and abnormalities of the cervix can include: sexually transmitted diseases (genital warts, Human

Papilloma Virus, syphilis, herpes, chlamydia, gonorrhea, HIV, and AIDS), dysplasia (a change in cells on the surface of the cervix), polyps (benign, non-cancerous growths), cervicitis (inflammation of the cervix), or cancer (malignant tissues or growths in the cervix). Factors that place a woman at a higher risk for cervical cancer include: genital warts, HIV, AIDS, smoking, poor eating habits, and having multiple sex partners.

Treatment: To first diagnosis any cervical abnormality, a Pap Test and pelvic exam are given. These may be given annually to any woman who is sexually active. They may be required more often if the woman is having a problem and her physician recommends it. The Pap Test will help to detect abnormal cellular changes in the cervix. The results may indicate further testing, or a biopsy may be needed. The Pap Test, along with a biopsy or other tests, may help to confirm a diagnosis. If a diagnosis of cervical cancer is discovered, a hysterectomy is frequently required.

Word: **Colposcopy**
Definition: A magnification device that is used to obtain a closer view of the cervix, vulva or vagina.
Condition: A colposcopy may be recommended if your Pap test shows abnormal cells. The colposcopy may be used to help diagnose cervical cancers, dysplasia, genital warts on the cervix, and polyps. A biopsy may be performed at the time of the colposcopy to help identify the disease or type of cells that are being under investigation.
Treatment: The results of this test and any biopsies will provide your doctor the information needed to determine a treatment plan that is right for you. Different types of methods to destroy abnormal tissue may include: conization (a cone shaped piece of tissue is removed from the cervix), laser (a high intensity beam of light used to remove abnormal tissue or growths),

electrosurgery (heat is used to destroy the abnormal area), electrosurgical excision (the abnormal area is removed using a thin wire loop and electrical energy), cryotherapy (a probe coated with freezing agents is applied to the abnormal area), or hysterectomy (surgical removal of the uterus and cervix).

Word: **Constipation**
Definition: Difficulty with defecation, infrequent passing of stool, hard or dry fecal material.
Condition: This condition may be caused by a variety of conditions or diseases including, although *not* limited to: improper diet, postsurgical difficulties, certain drug interactions, or any variety of abdominal abnormalities or conditions.
Treatment: Your health care professional might recommend a change of diet to include more fruits, vegetables, whole grain cereals, and increase your fluid intake (extra water and fruit juices.) Some medication choices may include Milk of Magnesia or Colace to help with stool softening.

Word: **Cramps (also known as "Dysmenorrhea")**
Definition: A spasm or contraction of one or many muscles usually causing pain.
Condition: Cramps vary in intensity from mild to severe, and may cause nausea, vomiting, dizziness, backaches, abdominal pain and possibly diahrrea. Cramps can be caused by a variety of conditions or diseases including: endometriosis, pelvic inflammatory disease, uterine fibroids, and routine symptoms of the menstrual cycle. It is also possible to encounter pseudo-cramps after a hysterectomy or menopause. Pseudo-cramps are caused when a hormone is released and sends a signal to the uterus to contract. If there is no uterus, the muscles around the area where the uterus was contract, causing a "pseudocramp".

Dictionary Plus for WOMEN

Treatment: Pain medications such as Ibuprofen, Advil, Motrin, Tylenol, or Aleve may help. A warm heating pad placed on the abdominopelvic region can also help alleviate menstrual cramps. It is also recommended to avoid caffeine and chocolate during these times. In some cases, birth control pills may be effective in reducing menstrual cramps.

Word: **D & C (Dilate & Curettage)**
Definition: To dilate the cervix of the uterus and scrape and remove the lining of the uterus by use of a curette. (Curette is a spoon shaped surgical instrument).
Condition: This procedure is done to clean out the uterine lining. The results vary from person to person.
Treatment: This is usually done on an out-patient basis. It is usually recommended that the patient decreases her level of physical activity for 24 hours after this procedure. It is also recommended to call your physician if you have increased pain, fever or abnormal bleeding after this procedure.

Word: **Diarrhea**
Definition: Frequent passing of abnormally watery bowel movements.
Condition: It is a symptom of a gastrointestinal disturbance which may be caused bay a variety of conditions or diseases including, although *not* limited to: certain medications, gastrointestinal upset or infections, nervous disorders, abdominal cramping, premenstrual syndrome, bacteria or parasites, irritable bowel syndrome, Crohn's disease, or overuse of caffeine or alcohol.
Treatment: The BRAT diet includes Bananas, Rice, Applesauce, and Toast. It is advised to avoid coffee, milk or any caffeinated beverages until the diarrhea has stopped for 24 hours. Ask your doctor or pharmacist if over-the-counter medications such as Imodium AD and fluid electrolyte replacement is right for you.

Dictionary Plus for WOMEN

Word: **Dysplasia**
Definition: Abnormal development of tissues, and abnormal changes in the cells of the cervix.
Condition: These cells are classified as: mild, moderate, severe, and carcinoma in situ.
Treatment: Depending on the severity of the dysplasia, treatment may range from observation to hysterectomy.

Word: **Endometrial Biopsy**
* See listing for "Uterine Biopsy" on page 65.

Word: **Endometriosis**
Definition: A disease in which the endometrium (the lining of the uterus) grows outside of the uterine cavity, where it does *not* belong. It may potentially adhere to the bladder, intestines, bowel, rectum, ovaries, or fallopian tubes.
Condition: Approximately 7% (5 million women) of reproductive age are affected. It may be noted by painful periods, heavy bleeding, pain during or after intercourse, or infertility. Laparoscopy is a procedure that is often used to diagnose it.
Treatment: Medications including oral contraceptives, steroids, and hormones sometimes temporarily help control the disease, although do *not* cure this disease. Depending on the severity, a hysterectomy may also be recommended as a surgical procedure to eliminate the disease.

Word: **ERT (Estrogen Replacement Therapy)**
Definition: A prescription hormone medication containing "natural" or "synthetic" estrogens.
Condition: Sometimes prescribed to perimenopausal and postmenopausal women during their depletion of estrogen to help alleviate the symptoms of a hormone imbalance. Some women who are at risk of osteoporosis, or women who may be experiencing

23

severe menopausal symptoms may benefit from estrogen supplements.

Treatment: Estrogen creams, patches, pills, suppositories, or injections may be prescribed to relieve some menopausal symptoms. ERT's are classified as "natural" and "synthetic" estrogens. Both forms have benefits as well as side effects. "Synthetic" estrogens include: quinestrol (sold under the brand name: Estrovis), diethylstilbestrol (also known as: DES), and ethinyl estradiol (marketed under various brand names). "Natural" estrogens include: Premarin (a mixture of horse estrogens and estrone sulfate), estropipate (sold under the brand name: Ogen), and estradiol (Estrace and Estraderm). Please consult your health care professional to discuss your ERT or HRT options.
* For more information see: HRT / ERT Information on pages 76.
* For more information see the word "Estrogen" on page 24.

Word: **Estrogen**
Definition: A female hormone produce mainly in the ovaries, by the follicles of the egg, and by the corpus luteum. (97% of estrogen is produced by the ovaries and 3% by the adrenal glands.) The word "Estrogen" actually encompasses three natural estrogens. These three and their percentages in the female body are measured at approximately: 10% estradiol (E2), 10% estrone (E1), and 80% estriol (E3). Together, these estrogens are responsible for the female characteristics such as breast development, feminine curves, and menstruation.

Condition: This hormone, when it occurs naturally within the female body, helps reduce the risk of bone fractures, decreases the risk of heart disease, lowers the incidence of stroke, lessens the chance of blindness, decreases tooth loss, lowers the risk of diabetes, interferes with the thyroid hormone, keeps the skin looking younger and healthier, keeps the vagina moist, decreases the chance of Alzheimer's disease, and lowers the overall mortality rate of women. The reason estrogen affects so many different types of systems in the female body is because estrogen receptor cells are found on most cells in the body including: brain, skin, bones, and genital organs. During menopause, estrogen levels decrease as much as 75% in a woman. The female body naturally finds ways to compensate for that loss. When a woman consumes more calories than needed, estrogen production increases proportionately. Nature tends to cause women to gain weight with age, so they can still manufacture enough estrogen to stay healthy and live long enough to raise their young. During the times when estrogen levels decrease in a woman, hot flashes, night sweats, vaginal dryness, and decreased sex drive may occur. Also, as estrogen levels decrease, the risk of heart disease and osteoporosis increases.

Info: Some common foods and herbs containing natural estrogens include: apples, alfalfa, barley, beets, cabbage, carrots, corn, cucumbers, garlic, green beans, red beans, soy beans, squash, oats, papaya, parsley, peas, potatoes, pumpkin, rhubarb, rice, wheat, and yams.

Treatment: When the estrogen level drops in a woman, if severe side effects occur, it may be recommended that an estrogen hormone be taken in its place, as a short term therapy. ERT (Estrogen Replacement Therapy) is one of many choices which might be prescribed by a physician. (These estrogens when made, may be plant based or animal based.) However, there is much controversy regarding the side effects. It is important for the patient to be checked regularly for any malignant changes.

* See HRT / ERT Information on page 76.

Dictionary Plus for WOMEN

Word: **Exercise**
Definition: The act of putting the body in motion.
Condition: Exercise benefits both physical and mental health. It helps to decrease depression, decreases osteoporosis, increases cardiovascular (heart) health, increases circulation, and increases memory. Regular exercise helps to maintain strength and stamina, build muscle tone, and reduce anxiety. According to the American Heart Association, physically active women have a 60% to 75% lower risk of cardiovascular disease than those who do *not* exercise on a regular basis.
Treatment: Walking, swimming, biking, dancing, and aerobics are excellent forms of exercise. The American Heart Association recommends starting off slowly and gradually build up to a routine, aiming for 30 minutes of exercise 3 to 4 times per week, and be sure to consult your doctor before starting a new exercise program.

Word: **Eyes**
Definition: The organ used for vision and sight.
Condition: Over ten million Americans suffer from dry eye syndrome. By the time a woman reaches age 65, her body produces 60% less oil, causing the watery tear film layer on the eye to evaporate much faster, creating dry areas on the cornea. Dry eye syndrome is a common optic problem for menopausal women, due to hormonal changes. It can also increase in severity when using estrogen replacement therapy. Dry eye syndrome may also include: swollen or red eyelids, burning or itching eyes, decrease in visual acuity, and focusing difficulties. Dry eye syndrome may also be a symptom relating to rheumatoid arthritis, diabetes, thyroid disease, lupus, glaucoma, vitamin A deficiency, Parkinson's disease, dehydration, or previous eye surgery. Nearly half of all dry eye sufferers experience related symptoms involving the nose, throat and sinus.

Dictionary Plus for WOMEN

Treatment: Artificial or natural tears, such as Bausch & Lomb Moisture Eyes, may be used as a temporary treatment to soothe the symptoms of dry eye syndrome. Closing the eyes to rest, less computer use, *not* smoking, eating more fruits & vegetables, and drinking more water can also help to decease dry eye syndrome.
The American Academy of Ophthalmology recommends the following:
* individuals from puberty to age 40 who have had an initial comprehensive medical eye exam need to be examined only if ocular symptoms, visual changes, injury, or family risk for development of significant eye disease are present.
* at age 40, a baseline comprehensive medical eye exam should be done.
* from age 40 to 64, an eye exam by an ophthalmologist should be done every two to four years.
* from age 65 and older, should be examined every one to two years by an ophthalmologist.

Word: **Fallopian Tubes**
Definition: The tube which extends from the uterus and ends near the ovary. Each tube measures approximately 4½ inches in length and ¼ of an inch in diameter. Its function is to convey the egg from the ovary to the uterus, and the spermatozoa from the uterus towards the ovary.
Condition: Any disease or difficulty which may inhibit the tube from carrying out its function.
Treatment: Depending on the disease or situation, treatment may range from medication to surgery.

Dictionary Plus for WOMEN

Word: **Fibrocystic Breast Disease**
Definition: It is a diagnosis that is characterized by breast pain or tenderness, cysts, and noncancerous lumpy areas in the breast.
Condition: Fibrocystic breast conditions are found in approximately 75% of all women, ages 30 to 50. Fibrocystic breast disease is caused by an estrogen dominance. Most fibrocystic changes are not associated with breast cancer, however these fibrocystic changes usually make it more difficult to diagnose an early breast cancer. The cysts in the fibrocystic breast disease may be fluid filled cysts or solid fibrous cysts formed from connective tissue. They may become more painful or even grow slightly in size depending on the time of the woman's menstrual cycle.
Treatment: As a woman goes through menopause, fibrocystic breast disease usually decreases and sometimes disappears, due to the decrease of estrogen in the body. Other ways to lessen the symptoms of fibrocystic breast disease include: taking Vitamin E, Vitamin B6 and magnesium supplements, avoiding caffeine products, avoiding tea, avoiding chocolate, avoiding coffee (Since coffee is a natural phytoestrogen, even decaffeinated coffee may increase the symptoms of fibrocystic breast disease.), avoiding beer (Beer also contains phytoestrogens from the hops that are used, thus increasing symptoms of fibrocystic breast disease.), and increasing progesterone levels without increasing the estrogen levels. It is important to stay comfortable by applying warm compresses, wearing a good support bra, and take an over-the-counter pain medication if necessary. The best time to have a mammogram or a self breast exam is 5 to 7 days after menstruation, when breast tenderness and swelling are at a minimum. If you have any questions regarding the changes of your breasts, please contact your health care professional.

Word:	**Fibroid Tumor**
Definition:	Benign (*non*-cancerous) growths found in or on the uterus.
Condition:	They are tumors that may show no symptoms at all or they may cause severe pain, bleeding, and permanent damage to other organs. They can range in size from a pea to a grapefruit, or larger. They may grow slowly, or grow in spurts. A woman may have zero or many. Depending on their location, they may press against nearby organs causing a variety of problems, including constipation or urinary difficulties. A variety of exams may be used to diagnose a fibroid condition. These exams are: ultrasound, hysteroscopy, laparoscopy, MRI (Magnetic Resonance Imaging), and CT (Computerized Tomography).
Treatment:	Pelvic exams are usually recommended every 3 to 6 months, in order to monitor uterine fibroids. Treatments range, depending on the size of the fibroid and the individual situation. Some medications may temporarily help shrink fibroids, but do *not* cure them. Endometrial Ablation is a scraping procedure that may be recommended in order to remove some fibroids. Myomectomy is a surgical procedure that removes the fibroids and leaves the uterus in place. A surgical procedure such as a hysterectomy may be recommended for some severe cases.
Word:	**Fosamax (Alendronate Sodium)**
Definition:	A prescription medication made by the pharmaceutical company: Merck & Co, Inc.
Condition:	It is used in the treatment and prevention of osteoporosis in some post menopausal women. It works by reducing the activity of the cells that cause bone loss, and increasing the amount of bone in most patients.
Treatment:	As with all prescription medications, there are benefits as well as side effects. Possible side effects include:

severe digestive reactions, irritation, inflammation, and ulcerations of the esophagus and digestive tract, and constipation. These reactions can cause chest pain, heart burn, internal bleeding, and pain when swallowing. You must speak with your health care professional to see if this medication is right for you.

Word:	**F.S.H. (Follicle Stimulating Hormone)**
Definition:	A hormone that is secreted by the pituitary gland which causes a woman's ovary to release an egg.
Condition:	An F.S.H. level of 40 MIU/ML or greater indicates that a woman may be at the onset of menopause. F.S.H. may also indirectly dilate blood vessels that lie beneath the skin. Dilating a blood vessel can produce a feeling of warmth and may be a cause of hot flashes and night sweats.
Treatment:	This is a blood test. The test measures the amount of F.S.H. that a woman produces. It provides the physician important information to help diagnose and treat the patient.

Word:	**Glucosamine**
Definition:	It is an over-the-counter dietary supplement, that has been noted for its positive effects for arthritis treatment.

* For more information, see the word "Glucosamine" listed in the Mineral section on page 99.

Word:	**Gynecologist (OB/GYN)**
Definition:	A physician with a degree beyond medical school who specializes in the health care of women.
Condition:	A gynecologist is a licensed physician who may diagnose and treat problems of the female system for a variety of conditions including (although *not* limited to): sexually transmitted disease, pregnancy, diseases of the breasts and reproductive organs, menopause, abnormal bleeding, and for a woman's annual physical exam.

Dictionary Plus for WOMEN

Treatment: Any woman who becomes sexually active, or over the age of 18 should see her gynecologist for an annual physical that includes a pap test and breast exam.

Word: **Hair**
Definition: A thread-like outgrowth from the surface of the skin.
Condition: Physical conditions such as menopause can cause the hair to become thinner and dryer. The decrease in estrogen can also cause an increase in facial hair.
Treatment: For the hair on your head: hair care products such as conditioners, and volumizers may help some. It is increasingly important *not* to over dry your hair by using hot hair dryers, curling irons, or perming products. Do *not* over use hair sprays, gels and mousse that can dry out and damage your hair. For the facial hair: clipping with a scissors or tweezing it out are most effective as a temporary fix.

Word: **Headache (also see the word "Migraine")**
Definition: Pain located in the head. Different types of headaches include: Cluster Headaches, Migraines, and Tension Headaches.
Condition: Headaches may be caused by a variety of conditions including: stress, hormonal changes, high blood pressure, poor eating habits, too much sugar or caffeine, or pulled muscles in the back, shoulder or neck.
Treatment: Headaches may be reduced by relaxation, sleep, proper eating habits, meditation, massage therapy, acupuncture, or oxygen therapy. Some headaches require medication to relieve the pain. If a severe headache persists, call your health care professional immediately.

Word: **Healing Process**
Definition: The time that it takes for the body to recover after surgery.

Dictionary Plus for WOMEN

Condition: Hysterectomy, oophorectomy, or reconstruction of prolapsed bladder or uterus.

Treatment: Time: The healing process takes time. Don't expect after a 6 week recovery period that you will feel back to 100%. It may take up to six months before a woman can settle into her new form of what "normal" is.

Patience: It is frustrating not being able to perform your routine daily functions. It is now that you need a friend, relative, or co-worker (particularly one who has been through a similar surgery) that you can talk to, ask advice or questions to, and discuss and share experiences.

Exercise: Walking and gentle exercises, that your physician will tell you about, are necessary to help reduce the risk of post-surgical blood clots from forming. Gentle exercises also help to enhance a person's spirits and promote healing.

Rest: Everybody needs rest, and a person recovering from a surgery needs even more. Limit visitors and their length of stay.

Eating Healthy: Nutritious and healthy meals are crucial for proper healing to take place.

Doctor's Advice: It is important that you return to your post-surgical (follow up) appointments. It is at this time that you should discuss hormone replacement medications, alternative types of treatment, vitamin and mineral supplements, and any other questions you may have.

Word: **Heart Attack**

Definition: When one or more of the arteries that supplies blood to the heart is blocked. Depending on the amount of damage caused by the blockage, death may possibly result.

Condition: According to the American Heart Association, approximately 35% of heart attacks in women go *un*noticed or *un*reported. It is important to recognize the symptoms which may include any or all of the following:

1.) Uncomfortable pressure, squeezing, fullness or pain in the center of the chest that lasts more than a few minutes or goes away and comes back.

2.) Pain or discomfort in one or both arms, the back, neck, jaw, or stomach.

3.) Shortness of breath along with, or before, chest discomfort.

4.) Other signs such as breaking out in a cold sweat, nausea, or lightheadedness.

Risk factors associated with heart attacks include: smoking, high cholesterol levels, high blood pressure, overweight, *not* enough physical exercise, stress, diabetes, a poor diet, and being post-menopausal.

Treatment: Medical treatment must be obtained without delay. Call 911 immediately. Some physicians recommend to crush or chew and swallow an aspirin followed by a drink of water, if possible. Taking an aspirin immediately at the onset of heart attack symptoms may prevent the formation of additional small blood clots. This action may help to delay or prevent heart muscle damage and buy some time to get to the hospital. (Aspirins are *not* right for everyone, you must consult your physician before taking this medication.)

For more information, contact the American Heart Association at: Phone 1-800-242-9236 or on-line at: www.americanheart.org

Word: **Heart Disease (also known as Arterial Sclerosis or Cardio-Vascular Disease.)**
Definition: Any disease or difficulty of the heart that can shorten the life expectancy of a person.
Condition: Estrogen loss, high blood pressure, smoking, stress, overweight, family history of heart problems, poor eating habits, and high cholesterol are a few things that can greatly increase your risk of heart disease.

Dictionary Plus for WOMEN

Treatment: Quit smoking, eat properly and increase your fresh fruits and vegetable intake, and see your physician regularly. Some questions to ask your health care professional: Is estrogen right for you? How to start an exercise program for you? Where to find heart healthy recipes for you?
* For more information contact the American Heart Association at: Phone 1-800-242-9236 or on-line at: www.americanheart.org

Word: **Hemorrhage**
Definition: To bleed excessively.
Condition: Many diseases and tumors can cause increased menstrual flow. Some of the most common include: endometriosis, fibroid tumors, and cancer.
Treatment: Treatments will vary depending on the cause. Hormone therapies may be used to try to slow or stop the flow. Often times a hysterectomy may be needed in order to stop the bleeding completely.

Word: **Herbal Substances**
Definition: Also known as: herbal medicines and herbal remedies. These natural substances are made from parts of plants, trees, and roots for medical purposes. These natural parts contain varied amounts of plant hormones and plant steroids. It is these hormones and steroids, along with other active ingredients, that when orally taken, affect a person's physical or mental status.
Condition: These herbal remedies may be used to treat a variety of aliments. Some herbal medications may also help to reduce some of the symptoms associated with menopause.
Treatment: Herbal substances are available over-the-counter, and without a prescription. These substances should each contain information regarding the symptoms they are meant to alleviate, the side effects that may occur, and their recommended dosage. Before taking any herbal substance, you should speak with an experienced

herbalist, or a Chinese medicine doctor, or consult your medical physician.

* For more information re: Herbal Information, see page 79.

Word:	**Hormones**
Definition:	Hormones are substances that our body produces naturally within a gland, organ or part. These hormones cause a chemical reaction that create an increase in functional activity and increase secretions.
Condition:	There are many types of hormones that affect the human body. Each one has its own purpose. A deficiency of any particular hormone can cause side effects. Some of these side effects can include: infertility, hot flashes, night sweats, vaginal dryness, irregular periods, mood swings, and decreased sex drive, just to name a few.
Info:	NATURAL HORMONES include: estrogen, estradiol, progesterone, testosterone, cortisol, luteinizing hormone, and follicle stimulating hormone. (Progesterone made chemically from Diosgenin is progesterone, identical to that produced by the human body, therefore, can be termed "natural". Estradiol made by any pharmaceutical company is also termed "natural" hormone.) SYNTHETIC HORMONES include: phytohormones which are plant based hormones that have some hormone effect in humans, and xenohormones which are petrochemical compounds with some hormonal effects that are generally more toxic than natural hormones.
Treatment:	Hormone level testing can be performed by using samples of blood or saliva. Saliva testing measures the "free" hormones which make up 2 to 5 percent of the hormones in a woman's body which stimulate receptor cells and carry out the tasks they are designed to perform. Serum blood testing measures the "total" hormones which includes the "free" hormones and those bound to protein. If the test detects a deficiency

of a hormone, it may be recommended by the patient's physician to supplement that particular hormone with a natural or synthetic hormone medication. Some women fill their prescriptions and take what is prescribed. Some women have found specialty compounding pharmacies which create custom hormone mixtures, that provide blends, tailored for each individual woman. It is thought, that with these individual blends of hormones, that women will be able to obtain a maximum benefit while reducing their risk of side effects. And some women choose to let their hormones decrease naturally and supplement their health with vitamins, herbal remedies, or alternative therapies. Whatever a woman chooses, it is important for her to discuss all options, risks, and benefits with her health care professional.

Word: **Hot Flash (also known as Hot Flushes)**
Definition: A tingly sensation that flushes the body with intense warmth.
Condition: A hot flash is a symptom of menopause. 75% to 85% of menopausal women get hot flashes. Hot flashes can last from 1 to 12 minutes. Hot flashes are a normal part of menopause. They are caused from the decreased amount of estrogen in the body. Other influences that can increase hot flashes include: sugar intake, caffeine intake, emotionally embarrassing situations, stressful situations, vitamin and mineral deficiencies, and being over clothed in warm areas.
Treatment: Estrogen replacement therapy or hormone replacement therapy, a proper healthy diet, vitamin and mineral supplements when needed, and dressing in layers, all help to control and/or lessen the severity of hot flashes.

Dictionary Plus for WOMEN

Word: **HRT (Hormone Replacement Therapy)**
Definition: A prescription medication that is a combination of estrogen, progesterone, and (or) testosterone.
Condition: Sometimes prescribed to perimenopausal and postmenopausal women to help relieve some of the symptoms of menopause. HRT has been found to help alleviate hot flashes, night sweats, vaginal dryness, decrease the risk of osteoporosis, and possibly decrease the chances of getting Alzheimer's Disease.
Treatment: These combinations of hormones can be prescribed in the form of a pill, patch, cream, or injection. HRT has some benefits and many side effects. Please consult your physician to see if it may be right for you.
* See HRT / ERT Information on page 76.
* For statistics from the Women's Health Initiative study, see History: Timeline, July 9, 2002 on page 5, 6.

Word: **Hysterectomy**
Definition:
1.) Hysterectomy: surgical removal of the uterus.
2.) Total Hysterectomy: surgical removal of the uterus, and the cervix.
3.) Total Hysterectomy with Salpingo-Oophorectomy: surgical removal of the uterus, cervix, ovaries, and fallopian tubes.
4.) Vaginal Hysterectomy: surgical removal of the uterus through the vaginal opening.
5.) Abdomino-Hysterectomy: surgical removal of the uterus through an abdominal incision. The incision may be made vertical or horizontal.
Condition: Any variety of conditions or disease which may affect any part of the female reproductive organs. Some of which may include, and are *not* limited to: hemorrhaging, uterine fibroid tumors, ovarian cysts, ovarian cancer, cervical cancer, endometriosis, and prolapsed uterus.
Treatment: Whenever any type of surgical hysterectomy is recommended, it is important to follow your physician's pre-operative and post-operative care

instructions. It is common that a six to eight week recovery time would be advised with restricted lifting up to 3 months.

* For more information on-line, visit the 3 following websites:

http://www.besthealth.com/library/abhys.html

http://www.folsomobgyn.com/hysterectomy,_vaginal.htm

http://www.med.umich.edu/1libr/crs/abhys.htm

Word: **Hysteroscopy**
Definition: A long lighted tube, called a hysteroscope, is inserted through the vagina into the uterus. The uterus is then filled with a liquid or gas allowing a better visual of the area in question. A local or general anesthetic is often used for this procedure.
Condition: The hysteroscope is used to obtain a better view of the inside of the uterus to check for fibroids, polyps, the cause of abnormal uterine bleeding, and other problems.
Treatment: After the test is complete, the physician will discuss the results with you. With a diagnosis, your doctor can determine a specific treatment plan that best suits your needs.

Word: **Insomnia**
Definition: The inability to sleep.
Condition: This condition may be caused by one or a variety of reasons including: hormone imbalance (a decrease in estrogen can sometimes be related to the amount of R.E.M. sleep a woman gets), certain medications, caffeine, alcohol, cigarettes, anxiety, illness, restless legs syndrome, and people who work schedules that oppose nature.
Treatment: Eat a balanced healthy diet and drink milk, get daily physical exercise (outdoors is usually better), maintain a routine schedule that includes keeping the same wake up time and same bed time, sleep in a cool dark room,

avoid caffeine, avoid evening snacks with sugar in them, avoid alcohol, avoid cigarettes, or talk to your physician to see if hormone replacement therapy may be right for you.

Word: **Isoflavone**
Definition: A substance found in soybeans.
Condition: Isoflavones have estrogenic-like actions. It is believed that these isoflavones have cancer protective effects that work by inhibiting the growth of existing tumor cells. Isoflavones may also decrease the risk of bone loss and help to alleviate menopausal symptoms. Isoflavones have also been found beneficial at lowering cholesterol levels and improving overall heart health.
Treatment: Foods containing isoflavones include: soybeans, whole grains, berries, nuts, and flaxseed.
* For more information see the word "Soy" listed in the Herbal section of this Dictionary Plus, on page 85.

Word: **Laparoscopy**
Definition: A thin lighted tube (laparoscope) that is inserted through a tiny incision in the abdomen.
Condition: This allows a physician to inspect pelvic organs for endometriosis and diagnosis other causes of abdominal pain.
Treatment: After a laparoscopy exam, the physician will explain the results to you. With a diagnosis, your doctor can determine a specific treatment that best suits your needs.

Word: **Laparotomy**
Definition: A major surgical procedure that creates an incision into the abdomen. This surgery usually requires the use of general anesthesia.
Condition: This surgery may be performed in order to locate the source of the abdominal pain. It allows the surgeon to closely examine the abdominal organs including the

Treatment: liver, spleen, pancreas, intestines, stomach, and reproductive organs.
During the procedure, the surgeon may choose to remove adhesions, endometriosis, fibroids, polyps, and ovarian cysts. It is important to follow all post-operative care instructions that are given to you by your health care professional.

Word: **Liquids**
Definition: A substance composed of freely moving molecules.
Condition: Essential to receive adequate fluid replacement for the skin and body functions.
Treatment: Water and milk are most beneficial. Proper water intake is six to eight 8-ounce glasses per day. A woman in menopause should also increase her calcium intake by 500mg per day, for a total of 1,500mg. Milk is a great source of calcium. Soda pop is *not* recommended due to the amount of sugar and caffeine, which have been directly related to increased hot flashes and night sweats.

Word: **Luteinizing Hormone**
Definition: One of the hormones produce by the pituitary gland. (The other hormone is: Follicle Stimulating Hormone, F.S.H.)
Condition: It has the role of regulating the release of progesterone and estrogen in women. It is responsible for producing a large boost of hormone that is carried to the ovarian follicle which causes ovulation.
Treatment: If a woman has a deficiency of this hormone, it may be recommended by her physician to take a hormone replacement medication.

Word: **Mammogram**
Definition: A mammogram is an x-ray of the breast. It is advised that the patient does *not* wear underarm deodorant / antiperspirant during this test, due to particles that may show up on the x-ray film. During a mammogram,

Dictionary Plus for WOMEN

each breast is compressed, by a paddle like device, to spread the tissue apart to allow for better viewing and lower doses of radiation. The actual pressure lasts only a few seconds. It is best to avoid having a mammogram during the week before your period when your breasts may be the most tender. Usually 2 views are taken of each breast. A radiologist (a doctor who specializes in reading the x-ray films) will note any suspicious findings, and it is possible that some patients may be called back for additional views to be taken. The results of your mammogram will be sent to your physician, who will explain the findings to you.

Condition: A mammogram is a routine diagnostic test used to detect cancer, fibrous tissue (fibrocystic breast disease), and other abnormalities in the breast.

Treatment: A mammogram is *not* a treatment for breast diseases. A mammogram is one of the many tests that may be performed in order to help diagnose a disease, condition, or abnormality of the breast. Other forms of testing may include: MRI (Magnetic Resonance Imaging), breast biopsy, computerized tomography, and ultrasound of the breast. According to the American Cancer Society, women over the age of 40 are recommended to have a screening mammogram. It is also recommended for all women over the age of 20 to perform monthly self breast exams and report any changes to their health care professional. Early diagnosis is the most useful key for breast cancer survival.

* Also see the word "Breast Cancer and Breast Information" on page 18.

* For current guide lines and information about breast screenings, breast self exams, mammograms, breast cancer, mammogram screening coverage laws in each state, the use of computer-aided technology, digital mammography, and the use of MRI for breast screening in high risk women, call the American

Cancer Society at: 1-800-ACS-2345 or visit them on-line at: www.cancer.org

Word: **Memory**
Definition: The mental registration, retention, and recall of past experiences, knowledge, ideas, sensations, and thoughts.
Condition: Short term memory problems and difficulty with concentration are both a normal part of the aging process. Infections, illness, sleep deprivation, and stress may cause a decrease in memory function. If the patient, or family and friends of the patient, notice memory problems becoming common occurrence or concentration becomes frustrating, it is important to seek advice from a physician.
Info: Alzheimer's disease is a form of presenile dementia due to atrophy of frontal and occipital lobes. It may occur between the ages 40-60, however, it usually begins after age 60, and more often in women than men. It involves progressive, irreversible loss of memory, deterioration of intellectual functions, apathy, speech and gait disturbances, and disorientation. It may take from a few months to 5 years to progress to complete loss of intellectual function.
* For more Alzheimer's disease information, visit on-line at: http://www.alzheimers.org Phone # 1-800-438-4380.
Treatment: Vitamins B1, B6, B12 and Vitamin E are important vitamins for maintaining proper brain functions. (A lack of Vitamin B6 has been associated with increased levels of homocysteine, which in turn is associated with heart disease and Alzheimer's disease.) Fresh fruits and vegetables are very beneficial. Food high in MSG and preservatives may cause a decrease in memory function. Techniques used to enhance memory and recall include: working on crossword puzzles, playing simple memory games, reviewing simple math problems, or practice and repetition of any

Dictionary Plus for WOMEN

topic. Medical tests to determine brain functions and detect possible causes of memory loss include: CT scans, MRI scans, PET scans and SPECT scans.

Word: **Menopause**
Definition: A new phase in a woman's life that marks a point when she has *not* had a period for 12 months in a row. This stage is often referred to as "the change of life".
Condition: Menopause may occur naturally or surgically.
Surgical menopause is caused when a woman has a hysterectomy with the removal of the ovaries. Surgical menopause may causes more intense post menopausal symptoms. Natural menopause usually occurs between the ages of 45 to 55. It is when a woman's periods have ceased permanently and her child bearing years have ended. The ovaries get smaller, slowly stop releasing eggs, and produce as much as 75% less estrogen. This often causes hot flashes, night sweats, vaginal dryness, skin changes, and mood swings.
Treatment: Combinations of estrogen, progesterone, and testosterone may be effective in decreasing some menopausal symptoms, however side effects may outweigh the benefits, and therefore needs to be discussed with your physician. Other methods that aid in the decrease of menopausal symptoms include: eating a healthy diet, regular exercise, and adding soy to your diet.

Word: **Metabolism**
Definition: All the physical and chemical changes that take place in the human body.
Condition: The menopausal metabolism slows down, estrogen decreases, and weight gain usually occurs. The body has a more difficult time with vitamin, mineral and food absorption.
Treatment: Proper diet, exercise, and vitamin and mineral supplements are often required.

Dictionary Plus for WOMEN

Word: **Migraine**
Definition: An intense throbbing or pulsating headache.
Condition: Migraines are often associated with hormonal changes. Estrogen causes dilation of blood vessels and inturn may cause the onset of a migraine. These intense headaches are usually felt on one side of the head. They are often accompanied by nausea and sensitivity to light and sound.
Treatment: Prescription medications such as Midrin or Imitrex are usually the most effective. Occasionally, progesterone medication may be prescribed to decrease migraine symptoms and occurrences.

Word: **Minerals**
Definition: An inorganic element or compound that occurs in nature.
Condition: Minerals are essential for the health, well being, and production of all cells within the human body. Without a proper diet, a mineral deficiency may occur.
Treatment: Each mineral has a specific function in promoting growth and development and maintaining body health.
* See the Mineral section listed on page 97.

Word: **Mood Swings**
Definition: A wide variety of thoughts, feelings, and emotions.
Condition: Mood swings can include: irritability, fatigue, melancholy, and uncontrollable tension. Mood swings become a problem when a state of depression or psychotic type episodes take over.
Treatment: Exercise, proper eating habits, short term ERT or HRT supplements, *not* drinking alcohol, and getting the right amount of sleep that your body needs can all help to lessen the possibility of severe emotional changes.

Word: **Mouth (Dry Mouth also known as Xerostomia)**
Definition: When the oral cavity does *not* provide enough saliva and normal oral secretions to lubricate the mouth.

Condition: This lack of saliva in the mouth is a common problem for menopausal women. Up to 90% of all menopausal and post-menopausal women experience xerostomia. It is often caused by increased levels of progesterone in the body. Without the normal amount of saliva to rinse away food debris, plaque, and bacteria, a woman may be more prone to developing bad breath, gingivitis, an altered sense of taste, heightened sensitivity, and tooth decay. This dry mouth problem is also worsened by dry air, smoking, stress, anxiety, nutritional deficiencies, certain diseases (such as Sjogren's Syndrome, or endocrine disorders), certain medications (such as antidepressants, antihistamines, decongestants, pain killers, tranquilizers, or diuretics and cancer therapy drugs (such as radiation or chemotherapy).

Treatment: Sipping on water throughout the day, using fluoride rinses, avoiding dry or salty food, and stop smoking are the best ways to decrease dry mouth problems. Left untreated, the mouth may *not* have enough lubricants to wash away food and neutralize the acids, which can lead to tooth decay. Of course, excellent oral hygiene is essential in the care of the mouth. This includes: daily brushing the teeth, daily brushing the gumline, daily brushing the tongue, daily flossing between teeth, and visiting your dentist and periodontist as often as recommended by your dental care professional for routine exams, cleanings and dental care.

Word: **M.R.I (also known as Magnetic Resonance Imaging)**
Definition: Magnetic fields and radio waves combined with computer technology that produce an image on film.
Condition: This exam involves wearing comfortable clothing, free of zippers and snaps. All metal objects must be removed before entering the exam room. (Metals include: all jewelry, watch, hearing aid, metallic eye shadow, keys, credit cards, non-permanent dental

appliances, coins, any metal body piercings, and hair clips, just to name a few.) It may be necessary to cancel your exam before it begins if you have a pacemaker, surgical clips, certain implants, joint replacements, metal rods or pins or plates, schrapnel, permanent tattoo eyeliner, if you may be pregnant, or if you are claustrophobic. There are two types of M.R.I. scanners, an open M.R.I. and a closed M.R.I.. The open M.R.I. is like a short tube, opened on both ends, usually allowing the patients head and feet to stick out of the scanner. The closed M.R.I. is a longer tube that is closed on one end (sometimes causing a claustrophobic feeling), that the patient is placed into during the scan. In either type of scanner, this exam will have the patient laying on their back for 30 to 60 minutes while the scans are being performed. This is a test that may be used before a biopsy, or in conjunction with a biopsy to help confirm a diagnosis. It does this by detecting different densities in the body. Tumors develop their own blood supply and this unusual density of blood vessels pop-out on an M.R.I. scan.

Treatment: This is a diagnostic tool. It does *not* treat a disease. The physician will give the patient the results and discuss a treatment if necessary.

Word: **Myomectomy**
Definition: The surgical removal of fibroids, leaving the uterus in tact.
Condition: It may be used to remove small fibroids that have caused pain, bleeding or infertility.
Treatment: This procedure is *not* a cure. Fibroids may develop again, even after this procedure. It is also possible that this procedure may cause internal scarring that can lead to infertility.

Word: **Night Sweats**
Definition: When the body perspires with intense velocity while sleeping.

Dictionary Plus for WOMEN

Condition: These sweats usually occur after a hot flash. Night sweats can also happen during the day. Just like a hot flash, these are the result of decreased estrogen in the body. Other influences that can increase night sweats include: bed time snacks, sugar intake, caffeine intake, and too many blankets or pajamas with fabric that does *not* allow the body to breathe.

Treatment: Estrogen replacement therapy or hormone replacement therapy, a proper healthy diet (which includes *not* eating any sweet bed time snacks), and cooler bedroom temperatures, all help to lessen the number and intensity of night sweats.

Word: **Oophorectomy**
Definition: Surgical removal of one or both ovaries.
Condition: This may be necessary due to cysts, tumors, cancer, or other diseases. Once an ovary is removed, less estrogen will be produced in the body.
Treatment: This is a surgical procedure that is done under general anesthetic. Once one or both ovaries are removed, it is important that you discuss any hormone replacement therapy questions with your physician.

Word: **Osteoporosis**
Definition: A condition in which the bones become brittle and are more susceptible to fractures.
Condition: After menopause, women loose approximately 2% to 5% of bone each year for the first 5 years and 1% of bone loss each year after that. According to the National Osteoporosis Foundation, 1 out of 3 women will experience an osteoporosis related fracture in their lifetime. Hip fractures are the most serious. Approximately 25% of women with a hip fracture will be admitted to a nursing home and some will die from complications associated with the fracture. Another type of fracture that can occur is located in the spine of the upper back, just below the neck. When these vertebrae become weakened by osteoporosis,

compression fractures may occur (causing the normal rectangular shaped vertebrae to become crushed into triangular wedge shapes) causing a Dowager's Hump to form. This causes a reduction in height, change in posture, and severe discomfort and pain.

Treatment: A bone scan may be suggested by your health care provider to determine the density of your bones. This scan does *not* treat the disease, however it does provide important information for you doctor so that a treatment plan can be tailored for your individual needs. Some things you should avoid in order to decrease your chances of osteoporosis are alcohol, caffeine, and smoking. It is important to maintain a physically active lifestyle and a healthy diet that includes calcium and vitamin D and fresh fruits and vegetables. Check with your health care professional to see if they may suggest any of the following: Calcium with Vitamin D, Glucosamine, ERT or HRT, or a variety of other prescription medications such as Fosamax, Raloxifene (Evista), Tibolone, Alendronate, or Risedronate.

* See FACTS listing osteoporosis statistics on page 106.

Word: **Ovarian Cyst**
Definition: A sac-like structure, found in the ovary, filled with fluid or diseased matter.
Condition: An ovarian cyst can be harmless, causing only mild pain or it may be very serious causing severe pain, menstrual problems or infertility.
Treatment: Ovarian cystectomy (removal of the cyst) or an oophorectomy (removal of the ovary) may be recommended depending upon the extent of the problem.

Word: **Ovaries**
Definition: A set of glands, (one ovary located on each side of the uterus), that contains the eggs released at ovulation

	time. These two ovaries are also the source of which estrogen (the primary hormone), progesterone, and testosterone are produced. An average ovary is almond-shaped and measures approximately 4 centimeters long, 2 centimeters wide, and 1.5 centimeters in depth.
Condition:	Ovarian failure (also known as: natural menopause) occurs when the eggs in the ovaries run out / or die, creating a deficiency of estrogen and progesterone. This deficiency creates additional health risks for the menopausal woman. Some of these risks include: increased cardiovascular disease, osteoporosis, increased blood pressure, decreased memory functions, and increased risk of cancers. Other diseases and conditions of the ovaries may include endometriosis and ovarian cysts.
Info:	The risk of ovarian cancer increases with age. Ovarian cancer is the fifth leading cause of cancer deaths in the United States.
Treatment:	Each particular treatment would depend upon the specific disease or condition that the woman is affected with. Treatment topics that may need to be discussed may include: possible short term hormone replacement therapy, an oophorectomy (surgical removal of one or both ovaries), a total hysterectomy, or a total hysterectomy along with radiation or chemotherapy.
Word:	**Pap Test (also known as Pap Smear)**
Definition:	A medical test that checks cells from the cervix and vagina, in order to identify precancerous and cancer of the cervix.
Condition:	It is helpful if a woman can refrain from having intercourse, does *not* use tampons, and does *not* douche or use any vaginal medication, spermacides or lubricants for 2 to 3 days prior to having a Pap Test. These products and personal habits may interfere with the results. This test is done during a pelvic exam. A speculum would be inserted into the vagina and a swab

Dictionary Plus for WOMEN

or small brush is then used to scrape tiny tissue samples from the cervix and vagina. This sample is then sent to a laboratory for testing. The results can determine if you have cancer or other abnormal cells. Atypical cells are often caused by yeast or bacterial infections. Dysplasia cells may be precancerous. Hyperplasia is an increase in the number of normal cells lining the uterus. Although this condition is usually not cancerous, it may develop into cancer in some women. (A Pap Test will *not* usually detect hyperplasia and will rarely detect cancer of the ovaries.)

Treatment: This is a test that may help diagnosis a problem. It does *not* treat the problem. The physician will discuss the results with you. It is possible that further testing may be needed, such as a colposcopy, to help accurately diagnose an abnormality. The American Cancer Society recommends a yearly Pap Test and pelvic exam for any woman who is sexually active or is over the age of 18. This also applies to post-menopausal women who have *not* had a hysterectomy.

* For more information on Pap Test or cervical cancer, phone the American Cancer Society at: 1-800-ACS-2345 or visit them on-line at: www.cancer.org

Word: **Pelvic Floor Disorders**
Definition: Any disorder of the pelvic muscles, pelvic connective tissues, or pelvic outlet area.
Condition: Approximately 300,000 women each year cause harm to their pelvic floor during child birth. These injuries often result in torn or weakened muscles and ligaments, creating uncomfortable and embarrassing situations. Urinary incontinence (urinary leakage), bladder prolapse, and uterine prolapse are often a result of these pelvic floor disorders. These problems tend to worsen throughout time, during menopause, due to weight gain, due to prolonged periods of time standing upright, while lifting heavy objects, during coughing

	and sneezing, and while being intensely physically active.
Treatment:	Kegel exercises can help a person strengthen their pelvic muscles. Kegel exercises require a woman to contract her pelvic muscles gently as if she were attempting to hold back gas. It is a slight inward and upward tightening sensation. This may be performed several times each day and as often as necessary. Practicing this steady holding contraction, can help a woman advance to having the ability to cough and maintain bladder control at the same time. (Many women strain too hard and end up pushing down. This is *not* the correct way to do this exercise.) Biofeedback enables the person to improve pelvic muscle function through muscle awareness. Biofeedback, combined with a home exercise program, can lead to increased muscle strength and improved coordination. Prescription medication may be required for some individuals whom pelvic floor disorders are the result of other diseases such as multiple sclerosis, diabetes, or cancer, or for individuals whom these other methods do *not* work for. Surgery may also be an option when all other methods have been tried and are unsuccessful. Wearing absorbent pads or disposable under garments will also help to protect against leakage.
Word:	**Peri-Menopause**
Definition:	A range of time that may encompass 1 to 8 years prior to menopause. This time frame also include the pre-menopausal phase.
Condition:	Peri-menopause commonly occurs in women between the ages of 40 to 51. However, these hormonal changes may start as early as a woman's late 30's. These physical and emotional changes occur as a direct result of fluctuating levels of estrogen. During this time a woman is still fertile and could possibly become pregnant. The most common symptoms at this stage include: vaginal dryness and a decreased libido.

	Occasionally irregular menstrual cycles and hot flashes may occur.
Treatment:	It is generally recommended to decrease salt, sugar, and caffeine consumption. Regular physical exercise is also encouraged. Provided the woman is *not* pregnant, some physicians may prescribe a short term hormone replacement therapy or oral contraceptives to help decrease the symptoms of mood swings, hot flashes, and irregular periods. Vitamin E and Vitamin B6 supplements may also be recommended.
Word:	**Period (Menstrual Cycle)**
Definition:	An average 28 day cycle in a woman's life that provides a reoccurring series of hormonal changes in the reproductive system. The period occurs when the uterus sheds the endometrium, releasing the uterine blood. The average period lasts 4 to 6 days in length.
Condition:	It is normal for a woman's menstrual cycle to vary in length, in quantity, and in frequency from month to month. It is important for a woman to keep tract of her periods from month to month to learn what her individual "normal" may be. During perimenopause and premenopause a woman's periods may become heavier or she may begin to miss periods due to the hormonal imbalances associated with the onset of menopause. There is a variety of other disturbances and diseases that may also upset a woman's routine monthly cycle and some of those may include: poor nutrition habits, caffeine, stress, endometriosis, fibroid tumors, thyroid disorders, and hormonal disturbances.
Info:	Toxic Shock Syndrome is a disease that can strike women who use tampons (especially super-absorbent tampons), menstrual sponges, diaphragms, and cervical caps. It is a sudden and potentially deadly condition that occurs when toxins or poisonous substances form from an overgrowth of Staphylococcus Aureus bacterium. Often times a high fever and vomiting will accompany this. The potentially fatal part may occur

when the body responds with a sharp drop in blood pressure that deprives vital organs (especially the heart and lungs) of oxygen. Seek medical attention immediately if you have any of these symptoms.

Treatment: Tampons or feminine pads are designed to collect the flow of blood. If a woman has any questions regarding her period, she should discuss them with a gynecologist, physician, or her health care professional.

Word: **PMS (Pre-Menstrual Syndrome)**
Definition: A syndrome that can occur several days prior to the onset of menstruation.
Condition: PMS can intensify with age, possibly due to the changes in estrogen and progesterone. The best way to determine if you have PMS, is to keep a daily record of your symptoms and compare them to the time of the month when your periods occur. This information will also help you and your doctor in formulating a treatment plan that works best for you. Symptoms may include: menstrual irregularity, depression, emotional tension, mood changes, anxiety, irritability, headache, breast tenderness, water retention, swollen extremities, and weight gain.
Treatment: Avoid or limit caffeine, simple sugars, alcohol, and salt. Exercise and vitamin/mineral supplements are helpful. In some cases oral contraceptives or hormone replacement therapy may be suggested to help decrease some of the PMS symptoms caused by a hormone imbalance.

Word: **Polyps**
Definition: Benign (non-cancerous) growths, usually resembling a mushroom or tree type appearance with a large bulbous top and a stem like projection that attaches to the affected organ or part. Commonly found in vascular organs such as uterine, cervical, nasal, colon, and rectal.

Dictionary Plus for WOMEN

Condition: Uterine and cervical polyps may cause bleeding, and may undergo malignant changes. For these reasons the polyps are advised to be removed.

Treatment: Surgical procedures used to remove polyps may include: D & C (dilation & curettage), resectoscope, or laparotomy.

Word: **Post-Menopause**
Definition: This refers to a stage in a woman's life, after she has had *no* periods for a total of 12 months.
Condition: Hot flashes begin to level off. The skin and vaginal area become increasingly dryer. The risk of heart disease, osteoporosis and cancer increases. Post-menopause is a permanent and irreversible condition.
Treatment: Short term hormone replacement therapy, herbal remedies, vitamin and mineral supplements, and proper diet and exercise can all help to lessen the symptoms of post menopause.

Word: **Premarin**
Definition: It is the trade name for an estrogen combination sold by Wyeth-Ayerst pharmaceutical company. The estrogens contained in this prescription medication are derived from the urine of pregnant mares. Approximately 48% of it is estrone which is natural to humans and 52% consists of various horse estrogens which are *not* natural to humans.
Condition: Women who experience difficulties during the menopause transition such as hot flashes, mood swings, and vaginal dryness may choose this medication as their means of helping them deal with these common menopausal problems.
Treatment: Premarin is a prescription hormone medication. It is often prescribed for treating the side effects of menopause. This medication has many benefits and many side effects. Please consult your health care professional to see if its right for you.
* For more information about Premarin, look on-line at: http://www.premarin.com/ForWomen/1070.asp

Dictionary Plus for WOMEN

Word:	**Pre-Menopause**
Definition:	A woman at the beginning of her journey into menopause. This stage in her life encompasses the 12 to 24 months before her menstrual cycle stops completely.
Condition:	Generally, a woman in her mid to late 40's who is experiencing irregular periods, with common symptoms of vaginal dryness, hot flashes, night sweats, decreased libido, mood changes, dry skin, and possible hair loss.
Treatment:	This tends to be the time in a woman's life when she seeks medical treatment for her menopausal symptoms. Some women take prescription hormone replacement therapy. Others find relief through alternative medicines that aid the body and the mind. All women should eat a proper diet and exercise regularly. Vitamin supplements can also help to lessen the effects of pre-menopausal symptoms.

Word:	**Prempro**
Definition:	A prescription hormone replacement therapy medication made by Wyeth-Ayerst Pharmaceutical. Prempro contains a combination of hormones: 0.625 mg of conjugated estrogens made from the urine of pregnant horses (Premarin), and 2.5 mg of synthetic progestin, medroxyprogesterone acetate (Provera).
Condition:	Prempro is the HRT that is on the front line of scrutiny, since the Women's Health Initiative halted a study, 3 years early, due to the serious side effects that occurred for women using this particular medication for a 5 year duration. * For the list of statistics regarding this study, please see the History: Timeline, July 9, 2002 on page 5, 6.
Treatment:	Each woman must talk with her own physician in order to decide if this hormone medication is right for her.

Word: **Progesterone**
Definition: A female hormone that is produced in the ovaries, corpus luteum, adrenals, and placenta. It is responsible for changes in the uterine endometrium during the second half of the menstrual cycle and signals when to slough it off.
Info: Progestins are synthetic compounds which have progesterone-like effects on the uterus. It was in 1938 that Dr. Russell E. Maker developed a chemical process that transformed diosgenin into progesterone. The source of this manufactured progesterone was obtained from the extraction of plant fats called saponins. A number of plants were used including the Mexican Wild Yam and the Soybean. One type of saponin called diosgenin closely resembled progesterone. It is this diosgenin, that is still currently used in the manufacturing process, that provides us with the synthetic progestins of today.
Condition: Natural progesterone, that the human female body produces, helps to protect against fibrocystic breast disease, restores sex drive, helps to normalizes blood sugar levels and blood clotting, helps to restore proper cell oxygen levels, helps to prevent endometrial and breast cancer, necessary for the survival of an embryo/fetus, causes the glands in the endometrium to secrete lubricating fluids, is a natural diuretic, improves new bone formation, and improves mental clarity and concentration. Progesterone may also affect mood swings and may cause headaches.
Treatment: For certain situations, progesterone therapy may be suggested. When progesterone is added to estrogen replacement therapy, it can decrease the chance of uterine cancer. Discuss your options with your health care professional. For more information regarding synthetic verses natural progesterone see the Progesterone Advocates Network on-line at: http://www.progestnet.com/documents/synthetic.html

Dictionary Plus for WOMEN

Word: **Prolapsed Bladder**
Definition: The falling or dropping down of the bladder.
Condition: Loss of pelvic tone can occur with a women's natural aging process and may weaken with each pregnancy and childbirth that she goes through. These weakened muscles and ligaments relax to the point where they can *no* longer support certain internal organs. A prolapsed bladder can cause urine leakage, feeling of pressure, and pain or soreness if the tissue is exposed from the vaginal opening.
Treatment: Depending on the severity, treatments may range from muscle tightening exercises (Kegel Exercises), or hormone medications, to surgery.

Word: **Prolapsed Uterus**
Definition: A downward displacement of the uterus, which may cause the uterus and cervix to protrude from the vaginal orifice.
Condition: The most common cause is due to weakened ligaments after child birth. Other causes include obesity, hormonal changes and a woman's natural aging process. It may often cause discomfort, pressure and urinary leakage.
Treatment: Depending on the severity, a supportive device called a pessary (a rubber disk that is placed into the upper vagina) may be recommended, or a surgical procedure such as a uterine suspension or a hysterectomy may be needed.

Word: **Raloxifene**
Definition: This is a Selective Estrogen Receptor Modulator, manufactured by the Eli Lilly pharmaceutical company. (Brand name: Evista).
Condition: Post-menopausal women who have risk factors of developing osteoporosis or currently have osteoporosis may possibly benefit from this medication. This prescription medication is *not* an estrogen or a hormone. However, studies have shown that it

provides positive effects on the bones, heart, and cholesterol much the same way as estrogen does, without the negative effects that an estrogen would have on the uterus and breasts. Side effects of this medication may include: hot flashes, leg cramps, and blood clots. Each woman should discuss the risks vs. benefits with her physician to decide if it is right for her.

Treatment: This medication was approved by the FDA in 1997. It may be prescribed to post-menopausal women for treating and preventing osteoporosis.

Word: **Resectoscope**
Definition: A slender telescope with an electrical wire loop or rollerball tip.
Condition: Small uterine fibroids and polyps that require removal, may find themselves at the tip of a resectoscope, for the purpose of elimination.
Treatment: The tip of the resectoscope is used to cut off, cauterize, and destroy the affected tissue inside the uterus, that had posed previous complications or difficulties for the female patient.

Word: **S.E.R.M. (Selective Estrogen Receptor Modulator)**
Definition: A SERM is characterized by its positive estrogen like effects in some tissues with its negative estrogen like effects in other tissues.
Condition: SERMS are manufactured by pharmaceutical companies. They are currently being used to treat osteoporosis, menopausal health, and cancer.
Treatment: The first SERM to be developed was Tamoxifen. It has been used to treat breast cancer for many years. Raloxifene was the second SERM to be developed. Initially for breast cancer, during research, scientists discovered it had a positive effect on bones. Focus then switched to its use as a medication to treat osteoporosis.

Dictionary Plus for WOMEN

Word: **Sexual Relations**
Definition: A physical act of intercourse.
Condition: Any medical condition or disease that may change a persons physical or psychological ability to have a satisfying sexual relationship.
Treatment: Time, patience, and privacy are important factors in learning to adjust to menopause, hysterectomy, or any surgery involving the reproductive organs. You should talk with your doctor about any concerns you may have.

Word: **Skin**
Definition: The outer most surface of the body.
Condition: The most common problem during menopause is that the skin may become less elastic, and more dry, causing wrinkling, sagginess, dehydration, dermatitis, formation of larger pores, and loss of muscle tone, due to the decrease of estrogen. Skin cancers become more of a concern because the body becomes more susceptible to damage from the sun's rays and from any toxic environmental effects. Other physical problems that may show up as skin changes at any time in a person's life can include: anemia, cancer, physical illness, lung diseases, or asthma. Another noticeable skin change can occur at the onset of a hotflash, temporarily changing the color of the skin to a visible pink or red.
Info: Skin Cancer Information:
Most common risk factors for developing skin cancer include: chronic exposure to the sun, history of severe sun burn, having light skin color, having the presence of moles and freckles, and having a family history of skin cancer. Most common places for skin cancers to occur are on the face, head, neck and shoulders, usually as the result of sun damage.
* Actinic Keratoses are precancerous lesions that develop on chronically sun-damaged skin. They often

appear as rough, red or brown, scaly patches and may progress to squamous cell carcinoma.

* Basal Cell Carcinoma is the most common form of skin cancer. It often appears as a smooth, shiny growth that may have a bleeding center. It is usually slow growing. Often located on the face. Anyone who develops one, is often likely to develop more.

* Squamous Cell Carcinoma is often a light colored lesion (pink or tan color) with a flat, scaly, warty or sandpaper- type appearance. It may also resemble psoriasis or eczema. It sometimes arises on skin that has been scarred from previous injury or burn. These skin changes become increasingly common as a woman gets older.

* Melanoma is the deadliest form of skin cancer. It often begins as a dark brown, black, or multicolored mole or patch with irregular edges. Check for changes in size, shape, color, a new growth, and / or a sore that doesn't heal.

Check with your health care professional if you notice any suspicious looking growths anywhere on yourself. For more information about skin cancer, please contact:
American Cancer Society: Phone # 1-800-ACS-2345
American Cancer Society, on-line: www.cancer.org
The Skin Cancer Foundation: Phone # 1-800-SKIN-490
The Skin Cancer Foundation, on-line: www.skincancer.org

Treatment: Sunscreens (with a 15 SPF or higher), lotions such as Jergens skin care lotions, and moisturizers such as Clinique moisturizing creams are extremely important in protecting the skin. To help lessen contact with the sun and other damaging rays, avoid direct contact from the sun between 10am and 4pm, wear a hat, dress in light layers of clothing, and avoid artificial sources of tanning such as sun tanning lamps, sun tanning booths, and sun tanning creams. Exercise and healthy foods

Dictionary Plus for WOMEN

such as fish, peanuts, milk and water all help to decrease dryness and keep the skin elastic. Using clear, glycerine soaps that contain essential oils and Vitamin E all help with the overall maintenance of good skin care.

Word: **Soy (also known as: Soya)**
Definition: Derived from the word "soybean", it is a nutritional source of isoflavones.
Condition: Soy is beneficial to many aspects of menopausal health. It also aids in the maintenance of cardiovascular health and in the well-being of the immune system.
Treatment: Soy may be taken in as a solid (food product), as a liquid (soy milk form), or as a supplement (pill form). For more information, see the word: Soy, listed in the Herbal Information section on page 85.

Word: **S.T.D. (Sexually Transmitted Disease) also known as S.T.I. (Sexually Transmitted Infection)**
Definition: A disease that is acquired through a sexual act with an infected individual.
Condition: Most common names of S.T.D.'s and S.T.I's are: AIDS, HIV, gonorrhea, chlamydia, herpes, syphilis, and genital warts (Human Papilloma Virus). Having a sexually transmitted disease or infection may increase a woman's chance of getting Pelvic Inflammatory Disease (PID), cervical cancer, ovarian cancer, or uterine cancer. Common symptoms of sexually transmitted diseases may include: itching, burning, painful urination, odor, discharge, sores, blisters, lesions, rash, swelling, abdominopelvic pain, and during some stages there are *no* symptoms apparent, however, the disease or infection can still be passed from the infected person to the receiving partner.
Treatment: The symptoms of a sexually transmitted disease may disappear, but the disease itself may *not* be cured or controlled without medical treatment and medication.

Dictionary Plus for WOMEN

If you suspect that you may have a S.T.D. or S.T.I., see your health care professional immediately.

Word: **Tamoxifen**
Definition: The trade name is Nolvadex. It is a prescription medication that interferes with the activity of estrogen.
Condition: Some breast cancer cells are 'estrogen sensitive' where estrogen binds to those cells and stimulates the cancers to grow and divide. Tamoxifen prevents the binding of the estrogen and stops the cells from growing and dividing, therefore, preventing or delaying breast cancer recurrence.
Treatment: Tamoxifen may be prescribed to treat both early and advanced stages of breast cancer. For more information, go on-line at: http://www.oncli.net/tamoxifen/ or on-line at: http://www.breastcancerinfo.com/bhealth/html/tamoxifen.asp

Word: **Testosterone**
Definition: Normally associated with the male species, testosterone is primarily produced by the testes. However, testosterone is also produced by the adrenal cortex in both men and women. Varied amounts of testosterone are also produced by the ovaries in women.
Condition: It tends to accelerate growth in tissues and is essential for normal sexual behavior. It also tends to create a more energetic and spirited woman. It is responsible for muscular development, facial and body hair, and deepening of the voice.
Treatment: Hormone replacement therapy including testosterone might be prescribed for women who desire renewed sexual function. Prescribed in pill form or injection form, taking testosterone may cause pimples, increased facial hair, thinning of hair on the scalp, shrinkage of the breasts, increased cholesterol levels, increased risk of heart disease, increased risk of certain cancers, and

weight gain. One must follow up with their physician, as recommended, while taking testosterone replacement therapy.

Word:	**Thyroid**
Definition:	A gland located in the neck, lying in front of and on either side of the trachea.
Condition:	This gland produces a hormone that regulates metabolism, heart rate and body temperature. Malfunction of the thyroid can cause menstrual irregularities and even infertility. Hyperthyroidism, also known as Graves disease, is when your metabolism roars into high gear. A person feels nervous, sweaty, heat intolerant and may experience weight loss. Hypothyroidism, is when you have an underactive thyroid. The thyroid will slow down causing a goiter to form. Hormone levels drop in the body causing fatigue, constipation, feeling chilly, weight gain, hearing loss, dry skin, puffy face & hands.
Treatment:	Testing for thyroid disorders usually includes a blood test with T3 and T4 panels. Your physician will use the results of these laboratory tests to determine the treatment that is best for your situation. Thyroid medications, iodine, and hormones, are usually effective in treating this disease.
Word:	**Trans-vaginal ultrasound**
Definition:	A procedure that uses sound waves to show a visual picture of different densities within the body. The transducer is placed into the vagina to provide a better view than if it were placed on top of the abdomen. It is often used in cases when the patient is obese or if the patient can*not* fill their bladder to the level needed to perform a routine ultrasound.
Condition:	This may be used to detect fibroid tumors, calcified tissue, ovarian cysts, and other diseases.
Treatment:	This is a test that may diagnosis a problem.

Dictionary Plus for WOMEN

It does *not* treat the problem. After the test is done, your physician will discuss the results with you. A treatment plan will be determined that will best suit your needs.

Word: **Ultrasound**
Definition: A device called a transducer is placed upon the surface of the skin above the area being examined. Sound waves travel through the transducer and bounce off of tissues from inside of the body. These echos are then projected into a visual picture showing the different densities of the tissues and organs under investigation. (Ultrasound exams of the reproductive system are usually performed when the patient has a full bladder, this allows better visualization of the internal organs.)
Condition: Ultrasounds may be used to detect or determine more precise information regarding: fibroid tumors, calcified tissue, ovarian cysts, breast masses, source of pelvic pain, infertility information, fetus information, and other abnormalities.
Treatment: This is a test that may diagnose a problem. It does *not* treat the problem. After the test is done, your physician will discuss the results with you. A treatment plan will be determined that will best suit your needs.

Word: **Urinary Incontinence**
Definition: The inability to control or prevent the escape of urine.
Condition: Sometimes caused from the stretching of muscles during child birth, a woman's pelvic muscles become weakened and have difficulty controlling the flow of urine output. This urine leakage can occur during laughing, sneezing, coughing, lifting, or other sudden movements.
Treatment: Kegel exercises are exercises that help to strengthen the muscles in the pelvic floor. It has been documented in the Journal of the American Medical Association that routine use of Kegel exercises can help to reduce the symptoms of urinary incontinence by 81%. Other

Dictionary Plus for WOMEN

ways to help manage this problem include: making frequent trips to the bathroom to eliminate a full bladder, wearing disposable under garments, and discussing other options with your physician or gynecologist.
* For more information, see the word: "Pelvic Floor Disorders," listed on page 50.

Word: **Urinary Tract Infection (also known as U.T.I.)**
Definition: An infection of the urinary tract. This may include any part or all of the following: kidneys, ureters, bladder, and urethra.
* For conditions and treatments see: "Bladder Infection" listed on page 16.

Word: **Uterine Biopsy**
Definition: A medical procedure in which a small portion of endometrial tissue is removed from the uterus.
Condition: The endometrial tissue is sent to a laboratory, and looked at under a microscope to diagnose uterine cancer and other uterine pathology.
Treatment: After the test, your physician will explain the results to you. With a diagnosis, your health care professionals can help to form a treatment plan that best suits your needs.

Word: **Uterus**
Definition: A muscular organ located in the female pelvis that contains and nourishes an embryo/fetus during pregnancy until birth. The uterus is a pear-shaped structure and located in mid-pelvis. It is supported in this position by the pelvic diaphragm and several ligaments. It is lined by a mucous membrane called the endometrium. The blood supply of the uterus is derived from the uterine and ovarian arteries.
Condition: Endometriosis, cancer, and fibroid tumors are potential diseases that can occur in the uterus.

Dictionary Plus for WOMEN

Treatment:	When the uterus becomes diseased, a hysterectomy may be recommended.
Word:	**Vagina**
Definition:	A fibromuscular tube which extends between the cervix and the outside of the body. The vagina is located between the bladder and the rectum.
Condition:	Vaginitis is an inflammation of the vagina. Possible causes for this condition may include, however are *not* limited to: chemical irritation, vaginal dryness, infection, frequent sexual activity, irritation from a foreign body (including tampons), hormonal imbalance, taking contraceptives, or taking hormone replacement therapy.
Treatment:	The treatment will depend upon the cause of the inflammation. See your health care professional for the medical treatment that is right for you.
Word:	**Vaginal Dryness**
Definition:	When the vagina becomes unmoist.
Condition:	Vaginal dryness may be caused by a decrease in estrogen or from the removal of the uterus and cervix after a hysterectomy. As soon as the natural lubricants are no longer there, and the vagina has lost its elasticity, the vaginal walls become thinner and less flexible. This dryness can cause pain during intercourse and can also be a cause of urinary tract infections that may occur.
Treatment:	Different methods to help improve a vaginal dryness problem may include: HRT therapy, K-Y gel topical lubricant, eating or drinking nutritional products containing Soy, and taking Vitamin E supplements. Talk to your doctor to find out the best treatment for you.
Word:	**Vitamins**
Definition:	An organic compound essential in small quantities for normal physiologic and metabolic functioning of the

Dictionary Plus for WOMEN

body. Vitamins are obtained by diet or dietary supplements.

Condition: Without a proper diet, vitamin deficiency disease may occur.

Treatment: Each vitamin has a specific function in promoting growth and development and maintaining body health.
* See the Vitamin section listed on page 89.

Word: **Weight Gain**
Definition: An increase in a person's weight.
Condition: Hysterectomies themselves do *not* cause women to gain weight, however the following three facts are the most common causes for weight gain after menopause:

1.) During menopause, estrogen levels drop as much as 75% in a woman. The female body naturally finds ways to compensate for that loss. When a woman consumes more calories than needed, estrogen production increases proportionately. Nature tends to cause women to gain weight with age, so they can still manufacture enough estrogen to stay healthy and live long enough to raise their young, during a time in which they are no longer capable of producing any more offspring.

2.) Weight gain after menopause is nature's way to protect the female body against injuries. The fat cushions the bones and joints that may otherwise succumb to osteo-related fractures during a fall.

3.) Menopause often causes a decrease in metabolism, which inturn may cause a woman to gain weight. However, becoming overweight or obese can complicate all health issues. Some of the most obvious include: heart problems, high blood pressure, diabetes, kidney failure, and joint problems with the knees, hips, and back.

Treatment: Exercise and a healthy diet to keep the weight gain within proper proportions. See your physician for an exercise and /or diet program that's right for you.

Dictionary Plus for WOMEN

Word: **Xenoestrogens (also known as Xenobiotics)**
Definition: Petrochemical compounds and other foreign substances with estrogen-like effects, that are generally more toxic than natural hormones.
Info: The major intake of xenoestrogens occurs with the intake of red meats and dairy fats. This is because some animals are given estrogenic substances to fatten them up for market, and the majority are exposed when they eat grains that have been sprayed by pesticides. These xenoestrogens that have accumulated in the animal's body, inturn, accumulate in our human body, specifically in our breasts, brain, and liver. These areas are then prone to all the same side effects that negative estrogenic effects may cause.
Condition: Problems caused from xenohormones include profound impact on hormone imbalance, reproductive abnormalities, increased cancers of the reproductive organs, brain and liver, infertility, and passing on reproductive abnormalities to future offspring.
Treatment: Xenoestrogens are difficult to avoid, although there are ways to reduce your exposure. Eat organic fruits and vegetables, do *not* use lawn and garden bug sprays, do *not* use plastics (some plastics emit xenoestrogens when heated), and purchase products in glass or cardboard containers (*not* plastics).

Word: **Xerostomia**
  * See the word "Mouth" located on page 44.

Medical Terminology Made Simple

Common Name:	Medical Term:
above	supra (or) superior
after	post
around, near, (or) beside	para
bad (or) difficult	dys
before	pre
behind	posterior
below (or) beneath	sub (or) infra (or) inferior
bladder	cyst
blood	hemat
bone	osteo
breast	mammo (or) mast
cancer	carcino (or) malignant
condition of	a noun ending in "ia"
destruction (or) breakdown	lys
disease	path (pathy)
displaced	pexy
fallopian tube	salpingo
fat	lipo (or) adipo
flow (or) discharge	orrhea
formation of	genesis

Dictionary Plus for WOMEN

front (in front of)	anterior
glands	aden
heart	cardio
inflammation	a word ending in "itis"
intestine (large)	colo (or) colon
intestine (small)	enter
joint	arthro
kidney	nephr
look into	scope
many	poly
middle area	meso
muscle	myo
non-cancerous	benign
outer area	ecto
ovary	oophor
pain	algia
period	meno (or) men
pus	py
resembling (or) like	a word ending in "oid"
side (to the side of)	lateral
skin	derma
specialist	ologist
stomach	gastro
study of	a word ending in "ology"
surgical incision into	otomy
surgical removal of	ectomy
surgical repair of	plasty
tumor	oma
uterus	hyster
within, inside, (or) inner	endo
without	a prefix beginning in "a" or "an"
woman (or) female	gyno (or) gyneco

Dictionary Plus for WOMEN

Anatomical Illustrations

Reproductive Organs
(Front View)

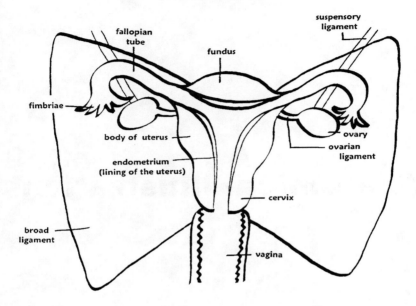

Basic Intestinal Information

- Rectum: posterior to the uterus and vagina.
- Anus: posterior to the vaginal opening.
- Intestines: superior to the reproductive organs, the intestines are attached to the posterior aspect of the abdominopelvic cavity by the peritenium.
- Small Intestines: approximately 21 feet in length. (includes: duodenum, jejunum, and ileum)
- Large Intestines: approximately 5 feet in length.

Ligament Information

- 3 ligaments hold each ovary in place:

    1.) ovarian ligament
    2.) suspensory ligament
    3.) broad ligament

- The uterus is held in place by the Pelvic diagram and several ligaments.

Dictionary Plus for WOMEN

Reproductive Organs
(Side View)

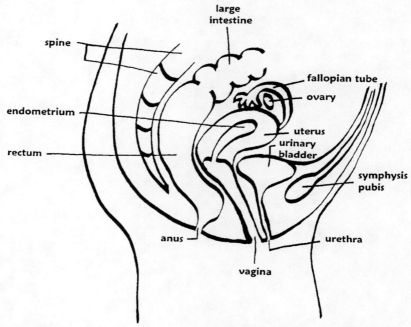

Urinary Tract Location

- Urethra: anterior to the vagina.
- Bladder: anterior to the uterus and vagina.
- Right and Left Ureters: anterior to the rectum and the spine.
- Right Kidney: posterior to the intestine, near the liver and gall bladder.
- Left Kidney: posterior to the intestine, near the spleen and pancreas.

Muscle Layer Incisions For Abdominal Hysterectomy
(anterior to posterior)

1.) Rectum Abdominis
2.) External Oblique
3.) Internal Oblique
4.) Transversus Abdominis

Dictionary Plus for WOMEN

HRT / ERT Information

Dictionary Plus for WOMEN

Hormone Replacement Therapy (HRT) and Estrogen Replacement Therapy (ERT)

Benefits of HRT/ERT	Possible Side Effects	Risks
• Decrease hot flashes and night sweats	• Breast tenderness	• Increases risk of breast cancer
• Improves vaginal lubrication	• Fluid retention	• Increases risk of uterine / endometrial cancer
• Decreases insomnia	• Occasional spotting	
• Decreases mood swings	• Facial discoloration (blotchy spots that do not disappear)	• Increases risk of cardiovascular disease
• Decreases risk of colon cancer	• Abnormal blood clotting	• Increases risk of heart attacks
• Decreases risk of osteoporosis	• Migraines	• Increases risk of stroke
• Decreases risk of hip fractures and vertebral fractures	• Nausea	• Increases risk of ovarian cancer
		• Increases risk of liver disease and liver cancer
		• Increases risk of gall bladder disease
		• Increases risk of blood clots
		• Increases risk of high blood pressure

Percentages of occurrences may vary depending upon the combination of hormones taken.

Prescription **ESTROGENS** include:

Premarin, Ogen, Ortho-Est, Estinyl, Estrace, Estratab, Cenestin, Menest, Ortho Dienestrol, Estring, Alora, Climara, Esclim, Estraderm, Estradiol, FemPatch, Vivelle, Delestrogen, dep Gynogen, Depo-Estradiol, Depogen, Estra-L, Gynogen LA, Kestrone 5, and Valergen.

Prescription **PROGESTINS** include:

Provera, Aygestin, Amen, Curretab, Cycrin, Prometrium, Crinone, and Hylutin.

Prescription **COMBINATIONS** of Estrogens and Progestins include:

Prempro, Combipatch, Premphase, Ortho-Prefest, Femhrt, Estratest, Activella, Depo-Testadiol, Depotestogen, Duo-Cyp, and Valertest.

Herbal Dictionary

HERBAL INFORMATION

Herbal substances are *not* recommended for everyone. Even though many herbal products are labeled as 'natural' and can be purchased over-the-counter without a prescription, does *not* imply that they are without side effects. Please be aware that any herbal medicines, herbal therapy, herbal remedies, and any herbal substances may alter or interfere with any prescription medications and any over-the-counter medications. (Including anti-coagulants, ERT's and HRT's, blood pressure medications, MAOI Inhibitors, heart medications, diabetic medications and insulin, and any vitamin and mineral supplements.) The use of herbs with the consumption of alcohol may change the toxicity to dangerous levels. Therefore, check with your physician or pharmacist before taking any herbal substances.

There are many physical and psychological conditions that may be altered in a negative way when using certain herbal substances. Some of these conditions include, although are *not* limited to: diabetes, high blood pressure, blood thinning or blood clotting disorders, kidney or liver problems/diseases, heart problems/diseases, pregnancy or women who are nursing, asthma or any breathing problems, intestinal or digestion problems, and arthritis. If you are aware that you have any of those conditions, or any other condition, disease, disorder, or any physical or psychological problems, herbal substances should be avoided.

Any herbal substance may cause serious side effects, permanent health problems, or death. Self medication of any substance is *not* recommended. You should contact your physician before taking any herbal supplement.

As of the year 2002, The FDA (Food and Drug Administration) states that herbal products can only be sold as 'dietary supplements'. Two reasons for this: 1.) Herbal substances are *not* regulated or approved by the Food and Drug Administration. The reason for this is because the amount of any active ingredient in a *non*-standardized herbal extract can vary from one preparation to another, making it nearly impossible to regulate. 2.) No single person, group, organization, or company can 'own' an herb. An herb is *not* a chemical that can be created by a pharmaceutical company. It is a natural substance growing in nature that no one has the right to claim as 'their own'.

Always use a variety of resources, research the herbal information thoroughly, research the manufacturing company of the herbal substance, and consult with your physician before using an herbal supplement.

* For more information regarding herbal supplements, visit: http://www.naturemade.com
* For more information regarding side effects and warnings about specific herbs, visit:
http://www.personalhealthzone.com/herbsafety.html
* For more information regarding the history and uses of herbs, visit http://www.holisticonline.com
* For other information contact the International Advocates for Health Freedom Act at: www.iahf.com

The herbal statements written in this book have *not* been evaluated or approved by the FDA. This information is for educational purposes only. The information and the products discussed are *not* intended to treat, cure, or prevent any disease or condition. Always consult your physician regarding the material and how it applies to your own personal situation.

Black Cohosh

Has been used for: treating many menopausal symptoms including hot flashes, night sweats, vaginal dryness, and PMS symptoms. It has also been used to reduce swelling, reduce cramping, decrease high blood pressure, decrease depression, decrease anxiety and irritability, reduce sleeping difficulties, reduce pain, and has been used as an antidote to poisons (particularly to Rattle Snake bites).

Info: The Cimicifuga plant is more commonly known as Black Cohosh. Other names it has been known as are: Snake Root, Rattle Root, and Squaw Root. It has also been sold under the trade name: Remifemin. This herbal medicine contains compounds that exert estrogenic-like effects.

Side effects: nausea, vomiting, headache, lowers heart rate, can cause uterine contractions, and can interfere with certain blood pressure medications and antibiotics. Long term effects and/or high doses may cause kidney damage and other serious side effects. This herb is *not* recommended for women who have had breast cancer because of its estrogenic effects.

Dong Quai

Has been used for: reducing bloating, calming menstrual cramps, regulating menstrual cycle, reducing headaches and high blood pressure, increasing circulation, relieving muscle spasms, and reducing hot flashes. It has also been used for treating insomnia and anemia, and has been known to have a mild laxative effect.

Info: Also known as Angelica, Tang Kuei, or the 'female Ginseng'. Research has shown that when Dong Quai is used alone, it has no demonstrable estrogen like effects on menopausal women. However, research has also shown that when it is used in combination with other herbal substances, it may result in a reduction of many menopausal symptoms. Dong Quai contains high amounts of Vitamin E and iron. It also contains niacin, magnesium, and potassium.

Side effects: Photo-sensitivity, dermatitis and possible gastrointestinal upset. Some Dong Quai preparations may act to increase blood flow and may lead to excessive bleeding, therefore it is *not* recommended for persons with fibroids or bleeding disorder. It may also increase blood sugar levels, therefore it is *not* recommended for persons with diabetes.

Echinacea

Has been used for: boosting the immune system. It seems to be effective in fighting infections of the upper respiratory tract, the common cold, and sinusitis. Research has also shown that it aids in decreasing inflammations of the skin and mouth, decreases occurrences of herpes, and helps to ward off flu viruses. It may also reduce the duration of runny noses and sore throats. It can stimulate wound healing and it helps to enhance the ability of cells to destroy harmful bacteria.

Info: It contains Vitamin A, Vitamin C, Vitamin E, copper, iron, and fatty acids.

Side effects: Individual who are allergic to ragweed or other plants in the daisy and sunflower families, or have an auto-immune disorder (rheumatoid arthritis, tuberculosis, lupus, multiple sclerosis), or an immunosuppressive disease (HIV, AIDS), or anyone taking any medication that effects the liver should *not* take Echinacea.

Garlic

Has been used for: its benefits to the cardiovascular system and decreasing cholesterol levels.

Info: Produces bad breath, heart burn, and flatulence.

Side effects: excessive bleeding and hemorrhaging, may increase chances of rejection after transplant surgery, and may pose problems for diabetic patients.

Ginko Biloba

Has been used for: maintaining mental alertness, improving concentration and memory, improving vision, promoting blood flow to the brain and heart, increasing circulation to the extremities, lowering cholesterol levels, and relieving chronic depression. It has also been used for treating ringing in the ears and dizziness (vertigo). Current research is being done to evaluate the effects of Ginko Biloba on Alzheimer's Disease and dementia. (That study is set to conclude in the year 2006.) For more information, see the August 2002 issue of JAMA.

Info: This is a natural blood thinner, therefore do *not* take with aspirin, Vitamin E, or prescription blood thinners. Do *not* take with MAOI (monoamine oxidase inhibitor) prescription medication.

Side effects: irritability, diarrhea, nausea, headaches, seizures, internal bleeding problems, and may cause negative effects on eggs and sperm.

Ginseng

Has been used for: helping the body to adapt to physical and mental stresses associated with hormonal changes. It has also been used as a memory booster, and to decrease fatigue.

Info: Vitamin C can interfere with the absorption of ginseng. Certain types of Ginseng should *not* be taken at bed time.

Side effects: headaches, insomnia, diarrhea, breast soreness and tenderness, skin rashes, asthma attacks, increased blood pressure, heart palpitations, or post-menopausal uterine bleeding. Do *not* take this herb if you are diabetic, have hypertension, or any bleeding problems.

Hawthorn

Has been used for: improving the circulatory system and regulating cardiovascular functions, reducing/regulating blood pressure, decreasing anxiety and stress, promoting sleep, decreasing insomnia, lowering cholesterol, reducing fluid retention, and decreasing night sweats.

Info: This herb has powerful antioxidant properties which play an important role in maintaining healthy heart vessels and promoting overall heart health. This herb is also a diuretic, which helps decrease the amount of water weight gain.

Side effects: Large amounts may cause lowered blood pressure, or fainting spells.

Kava Kava

Has been used for: improving sleep, decreasing insomnia, decreasing pain, relaxing muscles, lessening anxiety, and improving memory and concentration. It has also been used as an antifungal, antibacterial, antiseptic, and decongestant.

Info: The active ingredients in this herb produces a feeling of physical and psychological relaxation. This herb is primarily used as a natural sedative. On March 24, 2002 the Food and Drug Administration warned consumers about the dangers of Kava (or Kava Kava) causing liver damage.

Side effects: can cause liver damage, diuretic effects, hypertension, reduced protein levels, and blood cell abnormalities. This herb interferes with mood altering drugs such as Prozac, Valium, Lithium, and alcohol.

Maca Root

Has been used for: building strength and stamina, enhancing libido and increasing fertility, decreasing fatigue, altering blood pressure, increasing immunity, improving memory, and helping to lessen the chance of anemia.

Info: Also known as Peruvian Ginseng. It is a root vegetable related to the potato family. Is a good source of iron, zinc magnesium, calcium, potassium, phosphorus, and iodine. It is also rich in sugar, proteins, and starches. It has also been used in the treatment of Chronic Fatigue Syndrome.

Side effects: *Not* to be used in combination with fertility drugs, HRT or ERT, or with other libido stimulating drugs (such as Viagra).

Soy (Soya)

Has been used for: reducing hot flashes, maintaining a healthy heart and helping to prevent heart disease or stroke, stabilizing bone density, decreasing menopausal symptoms, regulating cholesterol levels, regulating blood pressure, regulating the immune system, decreasing mood swings, improving brain function, preventing illness, and may help to prevent some forms of cancer.

Info: The isoflavone substance within the soy bean produces a weak estrogenic effect. This inturn offers some of the same benefits as human estrogen without the dangerous side effects that prescription ERT's and HRT's have. Soy isoflavones also have antioxidant properties that help fight disease and decreases the chance of getting cancer. Soy helps protect the cardiovascular system against plaque build-up and helps to regulate blood pressure. Soy also helps to decrease the risk of osteoporosis. Soy beans are a good source of Vitamin A, K, E, and B. Soy beans are a good source of the minerals: potassium, iron, phosphorus, and calcium. Soy beans are a good source of the essential amino acid that form what is known as a complete protein. If you are a post-menopausal woman *not* taking HRT or ERT, soy foods or supplements may be a natural alternative to help alleviate some of the symptoms associated with menopause.

Side effects: If you are currently taking HRT or ERT, consult your physician before adding soy supplements to your diet.

St. John's Wort

Has been used for: calming tension, decreasing mood swings, and easing anxiety. It has also been used as an antibacterial and antiviral treatment.

Info: Interferes with the absorption of iron.

Side effects: headaches, increased blood pressure, nausea, vomiting, sensitivity to sun or blistering after sun exposure, increase heart rate, shortness of breath, and convulsions. It may also cause gene damage in sperm and eggs. *Not* recommended for people with high blood pressure, or anyone using an MAOI inhibitor or any antidepressant medication.

Vitex

Has been used for: decreasing menopausal and PMS symptoms, decreasing painful periods, decreasing tension and anxiety, decreasing fibrocystic breast disease, and decreasing premenstrual water retention. It has also been used to restore a normal estrogen-to-progesterone balance.

Info: Also known as Chaste Berry. It is thought to contain a progesterone-like compound.

Side effects: headaches, nausea, and skin rashes. It may inhibit the hormone prolactin and may increase the amount of luteinizing hormone, which inturn may increase progesterone. Do *not* use this if you are using ERT or HRT.

Wild Yam Root

Has been used for: increasing bone density, decreasing muscle spasms and painful periods, reducing inflammation, decreasing blood pressure, decreasing cholesterol, and decreasing fatigue and depression. It has also been used as a diuretic, expectorant, and a natural contraceptive. (Caution: using Wild Yam Root as a contraceptive may *not* be 100% effective.)

Info: Also know as Colic Root (because it decreases the symptoms associated with colic), Chinese Yam, or Bitter Yam. This contains a chemical called diosgenin, similar to progesterone.

Side effects: *not* recommended for women taking HRT, ERT, or progesterone therapy. It is *not* recommended for menopausal symptoms. It may cause temporary sterility.

Vitamin Dictionary

VITAMIN INFORMATION

Vitamins taken in moderation may be beneficial to a person's health, however, high dosages may cause serious side effects. Vitamins can't correct a poor diet, however, they can be used to supplement some of a person's nutritional needs. Vitamins should be taken with food for better absorption. You should always consult with your physician before starting a Vitamin supplement. (There are certain diseases and conditions that may create adverse reactions when mixed with particular vitamins.) It is important to read all labels for proper dosage and be aware of the maximum daily allowance.

Vitamins are classified into two groups: water soluble and fat soluble.

Water soluble vitamins are absorbed into the blood stream and excreted through the urine, quickly (daily). These Vitamins include: Biotin, Folic Acid, Vitamin B complex, Vitamin B1, Vitamin B2, Vitamin B3, Vitamin B5, Vitamin B6, Vitamin B12, and Vitamin C.

Fat soluble vitamins are absorbed into the lymphoid system in the intestines. In order for this to happen there must be fat intake in the diet. These Vitamins are stored in the body, and in the liver, for extended periods of time (varies per person, from days to weeks). These vitamins include: Vitamin A, Vitamin D, Vitamin E, and Vitamin K.

NEW VITAMIN INFORMATION: Recently, some manufacturers have added an ingredient (Polysorbate 80) to FAT SOLUBLE VITAMINS that make it easier to disperse in the stomach, although the Vitamin itself is still a fat soluble Vitamin. NOW LABELED AS A "WATER-SOLUBLIZED" VITAMIN, some manufacturers claim it may be easier for individuals with malabsorption syndrome to absorb the vitamin more easily in this new form.

The Vitamin, mineral, and herbal statements written in this book have *not* been evaluated or approved by the FDA. This information is for educational purposes only. The information and the products discussed are *not* intended to treat, cure, or prevent any disease or condition. Consult your physician regarding the material and how it applies to your own personal situation.

Biotin

Info: It is essential for proper body chemistry. It is needed for the metabolism of glucose and amino acids. It is also needed for normal hair production and growth.
Source: Cheese, egg yolk, cauliflower, and peanut butter.
Deficiency: A deficiency of Biotin may cause nausea, vomiting, dry skin, grayish skin color, drowsiness, loss of appetite, depression, and muscular pain.

Co Q 10 (Coenzyme Q 10)

Info: Co Q 10 is *not* a mineral, it is a coenzyme. It works with Vitamin E to fight free radical damage. It acts as an antioxidant against LDL (bad cholesterol). It improves energy production, heart health, and pulmonary function. It improves thyroid disorders, decreases hypertension, and decreases cholesterol levels.
Note: Individuals with severe heart disease or diabetes should consult their physician before taking this.
Source: Found in all animal and plant cells.
Deficiency: A deficiency of Co Q 10 has been linked to people with malnutrition.

Folic Acid (Folate)

Info: It is essential for the normal production of red and white blood cells and for the nervous system functions in the body. It is essential for the manufacturing of brain chemicals. It may also adjust hormone imbalances, revive a depressed libido, and may possibly help slow the bone loss that leads to osteoporosis. It plays a role in heart health by keeping homocysteine (bad cholesterol) levels down in the blood.
Note: Folic Acid should always be taken with a B 12 supplement.
Source: Green leafy vegetables, orange juice, liver, and sprouts.
Deficiency: A deficiency of Folic Acid may lead to premature gray hair, the production of abnormally large red blood cells, anemia, diarrhea, and nausea.

Vitamin A and beta-carotene (Carotenic Acid)

Info: It maintains general health and vigor of cells. It is essential for eyes, skin, hair, bones and teeth. It plays a significant role in antioxidant activity, and is needed for the production of estrogen. It may help reduce the side effects of aging. It also helps with the immune function.
Note: Too much can cause headaches, blurred vision, fatigue, diarrhea, irregular periods, skin rashes, loss of hair, and liver damage. According to the Journal of the American Medical Association of January 2002, long term intake and high dosage intake of Vitamin A may increase the development of osteoporosis hip fractures in postmenopausal women.
Source: Yellow and green vegetables, milk, and butter.
Deficiency: A deficiency of Vitamin A may cause night blindness, dry skin, dry hair, dry eyes, increased infections of the urinary, sinus, respiratory and digestive systems, and teeth and gum problems.

Vitamin B Complex

Info: The B Complex Vitamin is a balanced proportion of the following mixture: Bl, B2, B6, B12, Pantothonic Acid, Biotin, Folic Acid, Niacinamide and PABA. These are essential for healthy nerves, skin, eyes, hair, liver, mouth, healthy muscle tone

in the gastrointestinal tract, and proper brain function. These are involved in energy production and the central nervous system.
Source: Whole grain products, eggs, meats, and nuts.
Deficiency: A deficiency of Vitamin B Complex may cause fatigue, weakness, depression, mental difficulties, insomnia, and dry mouth.

Vitamin B 1 (Thiamin)

Info: It is necessary for releasing and producing energy in the body, especially in the brain. It is essential for the proper functioning of the nervous system and muscle coordination. It helps maintain proper mental function, especially in the elderly. It also helps to stabilize the appetite.
Source: Whole-grain products, eggs, pork, nuts, liver, and beans.
Deficiency: Common deficiencies of Vitamin B 1 include: anxiety, depression, muscle cramps, insomnia, and loss of appetite. Other deficiencies include: 1.) Beri-beri: is a disease causing partial paralysis of the smooth muscle of the gastrointestinal tract which causes digestive disturbances, skeletal muscle paralysis, and atrophy of limbs. 2.) Polyneuritis: causing impairment of sense of touch, and decreased intestinal motility.

Vitamin B 2 (Riboflavin)

Info: It is involved in carbohydrate and protein metabolism, especially in cells of the eyes, blood and intestines.
Source: Yeast, liver, beef, veal, lamb, eggs, whole-grain products, asparagus, peas, beets, peanuts, spinach, and mushrooms.
Deficiency: A deficiency of Vitamin B 2 may result in improper use of oxygen causing blurred vision, cataracts, corneal ulcerations, and dermatitis.

Vitamin B 3 (Niacin)

Info: It is involved in oxidation reduction, it reduces cholesterol levels, reduces blood pressure levels and assists in the breakdown of fat. It helps to maintain a healthy digestive tract and nervous system. It also plays a role in the maintenance of skin and proper mental functions.

Note: Too much could result in excessive hot flashes, ulcers, liver disorders, heart arrhythmias, and high blood sugar levels.

Source: Yeast, meats, liver, fish, tuna, chicken, whole-grain products, peas, beans and nuts.

Deficiency: A deficiency of Vitamin B 3 may cause dermatitis, diarrhea, psychological disturbances, loss of appetite, weakness, and vague aches and pains.

Vitamin B 5 (Panthothenic Acid)

Info: It helps convert fats, carbohydrates and proteins into energy. It is needed for normal gastrointestinal function. It plays a role in the formation of antibodies and the production of adrenal hormones which help to regulate nerve function.

Source: Kidney, liver, yeast, green vegetables, and cereal.

Deficiency: A deficiency of Vitamin B 5 may cause possible dizziness, painful or burning feet, digestive disturbances, muscle cramps, and skin abnormalities.

Vitamin B 6 (Pyridoxine)

Info: It aids in the removal of excess fluid associated with PMS and menopause. It reduces muscle spasms, leg cramps and hand numbness. It helps to maintain a proper balance of sodium and phosphorus in the body. It assists in the production of circulating antibodies. It is essential for protein metabolism and for the normal functioning of the nervous system. It is also essential for red blood cell function. It is required for hormonal balance and a healthy immune system. It plays a significant role in brain chemistry and function by helping to restore mental equilibrium caused from estrogen imbalances. It is also effective in decreasing the chances of a heart attack by preserving the elastic fibrils in the large arteries. It has also been shown to decrease the risk of degenerative arthritis, rheumatism, and tendonitis that is associated with the aging process by preserving the normal function of synovial fluid, cartlidge, nerves and tendons around the joints. It can also help reduce the pain and swelling associated

with arthritis. Vitamin B 6 is also a factor in the prevention of blindness.
Note: Too much may cause nerve damage.
Source: Salmon, yeast, tomatoes, yellow corn, spinach, whole-grain products, liver, yogurt, broccoli, and bananas.
Deficiency: A deficiency of Vitamin B 6 may cause depression, dizziness, impaired nervous system, anemia, convulsions, muscle weakness, slow learning, and dermatitis (eczema) of the eyes, nose and mouth.

Vitamin B 12 (Cyano-Cobalamin)

Info: It is necessary for the proper function of the nervous system and for the manufactering of red blood cells and certain proteins such as DNA. It has been known to decrease sleep problems and it plays a significant role in heart health by keeping homocysteine levels down in the blood.
Note: As we age, we have a lower amount of stomach acid secreted that is necessary for the absorption of B 12. Therefore, it is strongly recommended that people over the age of 50 speak with their physician about taking a B 12 supplement.
Source: Liver, kidney, milk, eggs, meat, and cheese.
Deficiency: Deficiencies of Vitamin B 12 are usually only seen in strict vegetarians, the elderly, or people with malabsorption problems. A deficiency could result in memory loss, weakness, lack of balance, mood changes, possible impaired nerve function, tingling sensation and numbness.

Vitamin C (Ascorbic Acid)

Info: It is a powerful water-soluble antioxidant that protects against damaging natural substances called free radicals, and supports the immune system. It works with your antibodies and promotes wound healing. Its major role is to make collagen (the main protein substance of the human body that holds the connective tissues together in skin, bone, teeth, and other parts of the body). It is also needed for the production of progesterone, and it aids in the absorption of iron.
Note: Too much Vitamin C can cause diarrhea and intestinal gas.

Source: Citrus fruits, strawberries, tomatoes, kiwi, grapefruit, oranges, lemons, lime, broccoli, and green peppers.
Deficiency: A deficiency of Vitamin C might cause Scurvy, anemia, muscle weakness, swollen gums, loosening of teeth, poor wound healing and bleeding problems.

Vitamin D (Calciferol)

Info: It helps build and maintain teeth and bones. It enhances calcium absorption.
Note: Too much might result in calcium deposits in body organs, fragile bones, renal (kidney) and cardiovascular (heart) damage.
Source: Sunlight, fortified milk, egg yolk, and fish-liver oils.
Deficiency: A deficiency of Vitamin D may cause soft, brittle bones and osteoporosis.

Vitamin E (Tocopherol)

Info: It is a powerful antioxidant that fights against damaging natural substances known as free radicals. It can improve arthritic problems, improve the immune system, protects against various forms of cancer, plays a role in maintaining a healthy heart and decreases the risk of a heart attack, and may delay the progression of Alzheimer's Disease. It helps to form red blood cells, muscles and other tissues. It plays an important role of keeping blood vessels open by controlling the fats that circulate in our system.
Note: Anyone taking blood-thinning medication should consult their physician before taking Vitamin E. Vitamin E should be stopped 4 weeks prior to any surgery.
Source: Fresh nuts, wheat germ, corn, butter, brown rice, soybean oil, and green leafy vegetables.
Deficiency: A deficiency of Vitamin E can possibly cause deterioration of cells and maintenance of cells. It may also cause possible nerve abnormalities.

Vitamin K (Prothombinol)

Info: It is needed for normal blood clotting.
Source: Spinach, cauliflower, cabbage, liver, and green vegetables.

Deficiency: A deficiency of Vitamin K may cause delayed clotting time resulting in an excessive bleeding disorder.

Mineral Dictionary

MINERAL INFORMATION

Minerals taken in moderation may be beneficial to a person's health, however, high dosages may cause serious side effects. Minerals can't correct a poor diet, however, they can be used to supplement some of a person's nutritional needs. Minerals should be taken with food for better absorption. You should always consult your physician before starting a mineral supplement. (There are certain diseases and conditions that may create adverse reactions when mixed with particular minerals.) It is important to read all labels for proper dosage and be aware of the maximum daily allowance.

Minerals are elements that are inorganic substances found naturally in the earth (but are *not* animal or vegetable). Minerals include: Boron, Calcium, Chromium, Copper, Flourine, Iodine, Iron, Magnesium, Manganese, Molybdenum, Phosphorus, Potassium, Selenium, Sodium, and Zinc.

The mineral, vitamin, and herbal statements written in this book have *not* been evaluated or approved by the FDA. This information is for educational purposes only. The information and the products discussed are *not* intended to treat, cure, or prevent any disease or condition. Consult your physician regarding the material and how it applies to your own personal situation.

Boron

Info: It is considered to help increase estrogen production. It also helps prevent calcium loss and bone demineralization.
Source: Alfalfa, apples, pears, grapes, nuts, legumes and leafy greens.
Deficiency: A deficiency of Boron may cause excessive urinary excretion of calcium and magnesium, inadequate estrogen production and retention, early onset of osteoporosis, and inadequate mineral metabolism.

Calcium

Info: It provides the formation of healthy bones and teeth, aids in blood clotting, assists normal muscle and nerve activity and cellular motility. It is recommended that Vitamin D be taken with calcium because Vitamin D helps to regulate calcium and phosphorus and aids in the absorption of these minerals into the bone.
Note: Abnormal conditions associated with megadoses can include depressed nerve function, drowsiness, extreme lethargy, calcium deposits and kidney stones.
Source: Milk, egg yolk, shellfish and seafood, green leafy vegetables, nuts, whole grains, and sunflower seeds.
Recommended Daily Allowance:
   * Women ages 25 to 50 before menopause: 1,000 mg.
   * Women ages 25 to 50 after premature or surgical menopause: 1,500 mg.
   * Women under the age 65, post-menopausal, taking estrogen replacement therapy: 1,000 mg.
   * Women any age, post-menopausal, not taking estrogen replacement therapy: 1,500 mg.
   * Women, all ages over 65: 1,500 mg.

Deficiency: A deficiency of calcium may cause osteoporosis, brittle bones, decrease in bone mass, stunted growth, poor quality of teeth and bones, excessive menstruation, nervousness, irritability, bone deformities, and possible hypertension.

Chromium

Info: This mineral is an unexplained factor in glucose tolerance.
Note: Too much can cause irritations to skin, lungs, and gastrointestinal tract. It can cause perforation to the nasal septum and can cause lung cancer.
Source: Brewer's yeast, wine and beer.
Deficiency: A deficiency of chromium may be one of the causes of glucose intolerance and peripheral neuropathy.

Copper

Info: Copper is needed to absorb and utilize iron. It is needed to help produce energy that the body runs on. It is needed for the production of collagen.
Note: Zinc interferes with copper absorption: People who take a zinc supplement may develop a copper deficiency if they don't also increase their copper intake.
Source: Oysters, nuts, eggs, whole-wheat flour, beans, beets, liver, fish, spinach, asparagus, potatoes, vegetables and meat.
Deficiency: A deficiency of copper may cause anemia and decrease HDL (good cholesterol).

Flourine

Info: It is necessary for the formation of healthy bones, teeth and other tissues. It is useful against infections.
Note: Too much can cause mottled teeth or brown spots on teeth.
Source: City water, whole grain oats, carrots, and almonds.
Deficiency: A deficiency of flourine may cause poor teeth development.

Glucosamine

Info: It is *not* a mineral. It is a carbohydrate substance manufactured by the body and located in the joints. Glucosamine helps make synovial fluid thick and elastic to cushion joints. In aging, we lose the ability to manufacture sufficient levels of glucosamine and therefore may benefit from a supplement. Proper levels of

glucosamine aid in joint function and joint repair. It has been documented in many articles, including the March 2000 Journal of the American Medical Association, as improving the symptoms in people with osteoarthritis.
Note: If you are diabetic, consult your physician before taking this. Do *not* take this if you are allergic to shell-fish.
Source: Glucosamine is made from Crabshell known as Chitin.
Deficiency: A deficiency of glucosamine can cause a weakness in the mucous membranes of the digestive system and respiratory tract. It may also cause a decrease in the synovial fluid of the joints. It can possibly weaken structures in the eye and in the heart valves.

Iodine

Info: It is essential for the production of the thyroid gland hormones.
Source: Sea-food, cod-liver oil, and iodized salts.
Deficiency: A deficiency of iodine can cause an enlarged thyroid (goiter), mental retardation, lack of concentration, poor memory, sluggishness, and inability to conceive a child.

Iron (Ferrous Gluconate)

Info: It is an essential compound of red blood cells and has a central function of transporting oxygen throughout the body. Iron makes up 66% of the hemoglobin in the blood. It helps to prevent iron deficiency anemia, which is the most common deficiency in the United States among women and children. Iron helps to strengthen the immune system and helps in the manufacturing of collagen.
Note: Abnormal conditions associated with megadoses can include damage to the liver, heart and pancreas. Large amounts of stored iron are associated with an increased risk of cancer.
Source: Spinach, broccoli, peas, apricots, prunes, raisins, oysters, clams, pork, liver, shell-fish, egg yolk, beans, legumes, dried fruits, pumpkin seeds, sunflower seeds, nuts, and cereals.
Deficiency: A deficiency of iron may cause anemia, fatigue, poor concentration, increase in colds and infections, headaches, and possible shortness of breath.

Lecithin

Info: Lecithin is *not* a mineral, it is a lipid. It is required for exporting fat from the liver. It is a substance that can change fat so that it becomes water soluble. It is linked to maintaining healthy cholesterol levels. It may improve brain function and enhance memory. It may help prevent heart disease and slow the aging process.
Note: Do *not* take this if you suffer from unipolar or clinical depression.
Source: Egg yolks, soybeans, and it is found in most plants and animals.
Deficiency: A deficiency of lecithin may be one of the causes linked to obesity.

Magnesium

Info: It is required for the normal functioning of muscle and nerve tissue. It is critical to energy production and protein formation. It's one of the body's major electrolytes. It assists in bone formation. It also seems to regulate the balance of calcium, sodium and potassium in our cells, particularly in our heart and blood vessels.
Note: People with kidney or heart disease should *not* take magnesium supplements unless prescribed by their health care provider. Other drugs that affect magnesium status are: diuretics, insulin, and digitalis.
Source: Green leafy vegetables, seafood, whole-grain cereals, almonds, pecans, walnuts, spinach, brown rice, corn, avocado, parsley, garlic, barley, bananas, potato, broccoli, cauliflower, carrots, celery, asparagus, green peppers, winter squash, cantaloupe, egg plant, tomato, cabbage, grapes, pineapple, mushrooms, onion, oranges, plums, and apples.
Deficiency: A deficiency of magnesium may be linked to diabetes, hypertension, high cholesterol, and blood vessel spasms. It may also cause possible gastrointestinal disorders, nerve and muscle irritability, irregular heart beat, personality changes, nausea, and vomiting.

Manganese

Info: It is needed for bone formation, hemoglobin, and inhibiting cell damage.
Note: Manganese poisoning is usually limited to people who mine and refine ore, causing neurological symptoms resembling Parkinson's disease or Wilson's disease.
Source: Whole grain cereals, green leafy vegetables, and tea.
Deficiency: A deficiency of manganese is extremely rare.

Molybdenum

Info: It is found in the liver, kidneys, bones, and skin. It is essential for the metabolism of iron. It might prevent certain types of asthma attacks.
Note: Too much can cause joint pain and swelling, nausea, and diarrhea.
Source: Milk, beans, dark green leafy vegetables, grains, and hard tap water.
Deficiency: A deficiency of molybdenum is extremely rare, usually only seen in people who have been on prolonged IV feedings. A deficiency might include rapid heart beat, rapid breathing, night blindness, anemia, mental disturbances, nausea, and vomiting.

Phosphorus

Info: It helps to extract energy, fats and starches from food. It is a component of healthy gums, teeth and bones. The remainder is found in muscle, brain cells and blood. It helps the kidney function and the heart regularity. It lessens arthritis pain and it helps to fight infections.
Note: Phosphorus needs Vitamin D and calcium to function properly.
Source: Dairy products, meat, fish, poultry, whole grains, cereals, nuts, seeds, eggs, beans, peas, corn, and soybeans.
Deficiency: A deficiency of phosphorus might cause weakness, loss of appetite, poor bone and teeth structure, arthritis, mental and physical fatigue, and irregular breathing.

Potassium

Info: It is an important mineral that helps maintain water balance and distribution, pH balance, muscle and nerve cell function, heart function, and kidney and adrenal function. It is needed for the conversion of blood sugar into its stored form glycogen. It also maintains blood pressure regulation.

Note: People with kidney disease should contact their physicians before taking potassium supplements. The following things can cause a potassium loss: alcohol, coffee, sugar, diuretic drugs, vomiting, and diarrhea.

Source: Bananas, oranges, apples, avocados, potatoes, tomatoes, broccoli, peas, spinach, parsley, lettuce, raisins, apricots, wheat-germ, salmon, sardines, and cod-fish.

Deficiency: A deficiency of potassium can increase blood pressure.

Selenium

Info: This is an antioxidant that prevents the accumulation of free radicals. It is known to stimulate the immune system. It plays a role in preventing certain types of cancers. It is involved in the production of the thyroid gland hormones.

Note: Abnormal conditions associated with megadoses can include nausea, vomiting, fatigue, depression, irritability, and loss of fingernails, toenails, and hair.

Source: Seafood, meat, chicken, grain cereals, egg yolk, milk, mushrooms and garlic.

Deficiency: A deficiency of selenium may be linked to a possible abnormality of the heart muscle (known as Keshan Disease).

Sodium

Info: Sodium Ions play a large part in transmitting electrochemical impulses to nerve and muscle membranes. It is also an important factor in regulating acid-base balance in the body.

Note: Too much can cause edema (swelling), hypertension, and cardiovascular problems.

Source: Common table salt, milk, eggs, carrots, beets, and green leafy vegetables.

Deficiency: A deficiency of sodium may cause dehydration, and heart and muscular problems.

Zinc

Info: It is necessary for normal growth and development. The immune system needs zinc to function properly. It is required for improving the sense of taste. It also has antioxidant activity.
Note: Abnormal conditions associated with megadoses can include masklike fixed expressions, difficulty walking, slurred speech, hand tremors, and involuntary laughter.
Source: Meats.
Deficiency: A deficiency of zinc may include impaired immunity and slow learning. An excessive zinc level may raise cholesterol levels.

FACTS

- Average menopausal age: between 45 to 55 years old.

- Estimated 1% of women go through menopause naturally before age 40.

- Hysterectomies are performed most often on women in their early 40's.

- Approximately 550,000 women get a hysterectomy each year.

- Approximately 20% of all hysterectomies are performed vaginally.

- The average weight of the uterus, fallopian tubes and ovaries of a woman 40 years old (without disease or tumors) is approximately 100 to 180 grams (less than ½ pound).

- Herbal treatments for menopause symptoms can provide some relief, however, side effects and risks must be considered before taking these herbal substances. (At this time, herbal medicines have *not* been approved by the FDA.)

- Between 75 and 85 percent of menopausal women get hot flashes.

- Hot flashes last on an average of one to twelve minutes.

- Studies indicate that approximately 25 percent of menopausal women are symptom free—no hot flashes, no night sweats, no vaginal dryness, no side effects from menopause.

- Menopause can make your LDL (bad cholesterol) level increase.

- There are 80 million Americans who have been diagnosed with osteoporosis. Nearly 80% of those with the disease are women.

- After menopause, between 25 and 44% of women experience hip fractures due to osteoporosis.

- One out of every three women (and one out of every eight men) will have an osteoporosis related fracture in their lifetime.

- Between the ages 70-80, women loose an average of 20-30% of their total bone mass.

- ERT / HRT helps reduce the risk of osteo-related fractures by approximately 33%.

- According to the American Heart Association, cardiovascular disease is the #1 killer of women in the United States.

- Before age 65, one out of nine women develop heart disease, compared to one out of three after age 65.

- Taking HRT for 5 years appears to increase a women's chance for heart disease by approximately 23%.

- According to the American Heart Association, each year, more than 11 times as many women die of cardiovascular disease as breast cancer.

- According to the American Heart Association, heart attacks are twice as deadly in women, than in men.

- According to the American Heart Association, One in ten women ages 45 to 64 has some form of cardiovascular disease.

- A study done at Harvard Medical School found that women who used talc on their genitals on a daily basis for many years were three times more likely to get ovarian cancer than those who did *not*.

- Ovarian cancer causes more deaths than any cancer of the female reproductive system.

- Women who have never had children are more likely to develop ovarian cancer than those who have.

- According to the American Cancer Society, approximately 23,300 women will be diagnosed with ovarian cancer in 2002 and 13,900 of them will die.

- A womans risk of getting ovarian cancer throughout her entire life span is 1 in 80.

- According to the American Cancer Society there are more than 1 million cases of skin cancer diagnosed each year.

- Approximately half of all cases of dysfunctional uterine bleeding (abnormal bleeding that is *not* caused by tumors, infection, or pregnancy) occur in women at the end of their reproductive years, ages 45-55.

- Fibroid tumors occur in 30-40% of women over the age of 40.

- Breast cancer is the second leading cause of death in women.

- Each year, 1 million women are told by their physicians to have a breast biopsy.

- 80% of all breast biopsies performed are benign, (non-cancerous).

Dictionary Plus for WOMEN

- Excluding cancers of the skin, breast cancer is the most common cancer among women, accounting for nearly one out of every three cancers diagnosed in American women.

- According to the American Cancer Society, about 77% of women with breast cancer are over the age of 50 at the time of diagnosis.

- According to the American Cancer Society, approximately 203,500 will be diagnosed with breast cancer in 2002 and 39,600 of them will die. (Of those totals, 1,500 breast cancer cases are MEN and a total of 400 deaths are MEN with breast cancer.)

- Taking ERT or HRT are major risk factors for developing uterine cancer. Also, beginning your period at an early age, going through a late menopause, or never having children may increase your risk of uterine cancer.

- According to the American Cancer Society, approximately 39,300 women will be diagnosed with uterine cancer in 2002 and 6,600 of them will die.

- Cervical cancer risk is closely linked to sexual behavior and to sexually transmitted infections with certain types of human papilloma virus. Women who have multiple sex partners are at increased risk of developing cervical cancer.

- According to the American Cancer Society, approximately 13,000 women will be diagnosed with cervical cancer in 2002 and 4,100 of them will die.

- Endometriosis is found in approximately 1/3 of all infertile women.

- Up to 95% of menopausal and post-menopausal women experience dry mouth, dry eyes, dry vaginal areas, or dry skin due to hormonal changes.

- Over 50% of women will seek medical intervention for their menopausal symptoms.

- Up to 30% of women who have suffered from Toxic Shock Syndrome will suffer a recurrence.

- According to the JAMA (Jan. 2002), Long-term intake and high dosage intake of Vitamin A may increase the development of osteoporosis hip fractures in postmenopausal women.

- Skin cancers affect one in six Americans during their lifetime.

- According to the American Cancer Society, facts for "2002", approximately 1 million cases of skin cancer will occur annually. The majority will be basal cell or squamous cell cancers. If these are diagnosed early, they have a high cure rate. Of these 1 million cases, 53,600 are expected to be diagnosed with a serious form of skin cancer called: Melanoma. Total skin cancer deaths are estimated to be 9,600. (This is estimated that 7,400 deaths will be caused from Melanoma, and 2,200 will be caused from other skin cancers.)

- Between 30% to 40% of all French and German doctors rely on herbal preparations as their primary medicines.

- Approximately 35% of American women between the ages of 15 to 49 have a pelvic floor disorder. Approximately 50% of American women over the age of 50 have a pelvic floor disorder.

- Approximately 30% of American women have hemorrhoids that were caused from the physical pressures during child birth.

- Six out of every 10 medications bought by consumers are over-the-counter medications.

- Cigarette smokers reach menopause approximately 2 years before non-smokers. This is due to the fact that the toxins they inhale cause follicular loss and earlier ovarian failure.

- Approximately ½ of all American women have a hysterectomy by the age of 65.

- One in 4 American women over the age of 65 has one or more spinal fractures.

- 45% of postmenopausal women in the United States take hormones for at least one month and 20% of them continue use for five or more years.

- Postmenopausal women taking estrogen only have a 60% greater risk of developing ovarian cancer.

- According to drug company estimates, (2001 year) approximately 8 million women in the U.S. take estrogen alone, and approximately 6 million women take a combined hormone replacement therapy.

- An estimated 40 million U.S. women will experience menopause during the next 20 years, and women today are living 1/3 of their life after menopause.

- Approximately 40% of women mention the difficulties of hot flashes, night sweats, vaginal dryness, and loss of sex drive up to 10 years after menopause.

Marketing & Manufacturing

The following contains researched information, views, and opinions of the author. It is unedited, and has not been approved by the FDA.

Menopause is a money making business. Millions of women look for anything that can help them lessen the side effects of menopause. With millions of women looking for new products, its no wonder everyone seems to want to jump on the band wagon to sell a product that they can profit from. So, it should come as no surprise to say that certain pharmaceutical companies have been in the top of the profit list for nearly 30 years, raking in multi-millions of dollars each year by selling millions of prescription medications to women.

Many drug trials are supported financially by pharmaceutical companies, searching for specific results. This is *not* a good thing. This provides the health care professionals and the public with a slanted view of certain products, causing a false sense of security. When looking for results of any substance, search for results that are performed by independent organizations who do *not* take funding from pharmaceutical companies, health insurance companies, or any other type of company that may influence the research and results.

All aspects of marketing are meant to target certain groups of people and to lure in perspective consumers. Same is true when selling any type of medication, prescription, or over-the-counter medication. The manufacture or company that is selling a product entices people by using clever phrases or a twist on words to hone in on their curiosity. Then they mix it up with medical and scientific jargon and throw in a few impressive statistics, and presto... they've hooked another customer. Sometimes even simple words lead you to believe their products are automatically good for you. For example products stating "for women's health", "healthy", "natural or nature", "bio-identical", "essential", "certified by", "approved by", "accepted by", "recommended by", "satisfaction guaranteed", and "decreases menopausal symptoms".

The words "Natural" and "Bio-identical" are the latest secret weapons with a single purpose: to confuse the customer.

Companies that use the word "natural" in reference to a hormone usually means that the hormone is taken from a naturally occurring substance in nature. Companies have the consumers believing this "natural" substance is naturally good for them. However, these "natural" substances can include anything from horse urine to wild yam. Yes, both of those are "natural" substances, however, estrogen in horse urine is a "natural" product from a horse and is "natural" for that individual horse. And progesterone derived from wild yam is a "natural" product from wild yam and is "natural" for the wild yam. Yet they are marketed as "natural" for humans, even though neither one is a "natural" human hormone. Humans have their own estrogens and progesterones that their own bodies deal with. Throwing in a DIFFERENT "natural" hormone is like tampering with a broken clock, sometimes it might fix it, and sometimes it might cause irreparable damage. Always take a second look at how these words are used in advertising.

Companies that use the word Bio-identical in reference to a hormone refer to the chemical structure being identical to that in the human body. But to make matters more confusing, Bio-identical hormones are often called natural hormones because they are made using naturally occurring substances in nature. These Bio-identical hormones are usually made in specialty compounding pharmacies using pharmaceutical-grade chemicals. They can create a hormone with an identical chemical structure as those found in the human body. This sounds great, however, we need to keep in mind that these hormones are chemically made, or derived from substances *not* found within the human body. These Bio-identical hormones may be an identical chemical match to a particular hormone, however, this does *not* mean that they will metabolize in the human body the same way that a human hormone would. It is the human body's complex interactions and its ability to recognize its own hormones vs. identical chemical compounds that can sometimes cause side effects or serious health risks.

In 1994, congress defined the term "Dietary Supplement" in the Dietary and Nutritional Supplement Health and Education Act (DSHEA). The act permits dietary supplements to be regulated as food, rather than pharmaceuticals. This includes: Vitamins, minerals, herbs and other botanicals, amino acids, and substances such as enzymes and metabolites. The FDA's Modernization Act of 1997 states that the FDA is responsible for proper labeling of dietary supplements and reviewing clinical research data. The FDA also evaluates the scientific evidence related to safety and effectiveness of the dietary supplement. It protects the public with reasonable assurance of the safety, sanitary, and effectiveness of dietary supplements. The FDA consults with experts in science, medicine, and public health, and in cooperation with consumers, manufacturers, and retailers to ensure public safety. However, even with all this FDA information, under the DSHEA of 1994, manufacturers and the dietary supplements themselves do *NOT* need to be registered or approved from the FDA before they are marketed. Currently the FDA issues regulations on good manufacturing practices that ensure the identity, purity, quality, strength, and composition of dietary supplements. At this time, the manufacturer is responsible for establishing its own manufacturing practicing guidelines to ensure the dietary supplements that it produces are safe and contain the ingredients listed on the label.

Prescription medications have some of the same draw-backs as dietary supplements in regards to being evaluated by the FDA. Before a drug is approved for sale, it is usually tested on thousands of people under controlled circumstances. If the testing is favorable, then the drug may be marketed. But all too often, the extremely serious side effects won't show up until hundreds of thousands of people have been using it, under a variety of situations and for extended periods of time. A General Accounting Office report stated: 51% of drugs cause serious side effects that are *not* detected until after they have been on the market. The FDA has the authority to temporarily remove or to permanently ban products that pose a serious threat to its consumers.

Women of today have been asked to take a more responsible role for their own health care decisions. Doctor opinions may vary, therefore it is extremely important that women digest as much information as possible, ask in-depth questions, and research the topics that are important to them. Women need to be able to weigh the pro's and con's to help make an informed decision about their health care.

Advice

Personal Advice From The Author

Before Surgery:

* Whenever possible, seek a 2nd or even 3rd opinion.
Make sure this is the right choice for you.
* Research, research, research.
Ask other family members or friends about their experiences. Learn by listening to other people's experiences. Read books and article about these topics to stay well informed about current choices, decisions and options.
* Quit smoking and drinking alcohol.
This may sound like a lecture… and it is. These only lead to more serious health problems and they can pose serious health complications during any surgical procedure. These vices also slow the natural healing process.

After Surgery:

* The healing process takes time.
Don't expect that after a 6 week recovery period you will feel back to 100%. It takes an average of 6 months before a woman can settle into her new form of what "normal" is.
* Treat yourself kindly.

I highly suggest that you ease back into your daily routine. Your body has been through a lot. You need to take care of yourself. If you feel the need to rest… than rest.
* Pay close attention to your body.
This will help to ensure your health and well being. Follow-up with your doctor appointments as needed, and maintain a healthy diet.
* Learning to deal with the "new" you.
This new stage in a woman's life can be both physically and mentally stressful. I highly suggest that you find some female companions: mom, sister, girl friend, female co-worker, or any woman who has been through this experience and talk to them. Ask questions, find out how they cope, or what has worked for them.

Important Resources

Alzheimer's Association
919 North Michigan Ave., Suite 1100
Chicago, IL 60611
Phone # 1-800-272-3900

Alzheimer's Disease Information
P.O. Box 8250
Silverspring, MD 20907
Phone # 1-800-438-4380
Internet: http://www.alzheimers.org

American Academy of Ophthalmology
655 Beach Street
Attn: Customer Service Department 495
San Francisco, CA 94109
Phone # 1-415-561-8555

American Cancer Society
1599 Clifton Road NE
Atlanta, GA 30329
Phone # 1-800-227-2345
Internet: www.cancer.org

Dictionary Plus for WOMEN

American College of Obstetricians and Gynecologists
409 12th Street, SW
P.O. Box 96920
Washington, DC 20090
Phone # 1-202-638-5577
Internet: www.acog.org

American Dental Association
211 E. Chicago Ave.
Chicago, IL 60611
Phone # 1-312-440-2500
FAX # 1-312-440-2800
Internet: http://www.ada.org

American Heart Association
4703 Monona Drive
Madison, WI 53716
Phone # 1-608-221-8866
FAX # 1-608-221-9233
(or) 795 N. VanBuren Street
Milwaukee, WI 53202
Phone # 1-800-242-9236
Internet: www.americanheart.org
(or)
American Heart Association
7272 Greenville Avenue
Dallas, TX 75231
Phone # 1-800-242-8721 (Any Heart Info)
Phone # 1-800-478-7653 (Stroke Info)
Phone # 1-800-694-3278 (Women's Heart Info)
Internet: women.americanheart.org

American Menopause Foundation, Inc.
350 Fifth Avenue., Suite 2822
New York, NY 10118
Phone # 1-212-714-2398
Internet: www.americanmenopause.org

Cancer Information Service
406 Science Drive, Suite 200
Madison, WI 53711

Centrum
Wyeth Consumer Healthcare Products
Phone # 1-888-797-5638
(or) Phone # 1-877-Centrum
Internet: http://centrum.com

Gynecologic Cancer Foundation
Phone # 1-800-444-4441
(or) Phone # 1-312-644-6610
Internet: www.sgo.org

Indiana Soybean Board
5757 West 74th Street
Indianapolis, IN 46278
Phone # 1-317-347-3620
Internet: www.soyfoods.com

International Advocates for Health Freedom
Internet: www.iahf.com

Mayo Clinic/Mayo Foundation
Women's Health Source
200 First Street SW
Rochester, Minnesota 55905
Internet: http://www.mayoclinic.com/aboutmayo/contactus.cfm

National Arthritis Foundation
8556 West National Ave.
West Allis, WI 53227
Phone # 1-800-242-9945
(or) Phone # 1-608-221-9800

National Cancer Institute
Building 31, Room 10A24

Bethesda, MD 20892
Phone # 1-800-422-6237
TTY # 1-800-332-8615
Internet: www.cancer.gov

National Institute on Aging
P.O. Box 8057
Gaithersburg, MD 20898
Phone # 1-800-222-2225
TTY # 1-800-222-4225
Internet: www.nih.gov/nia

National Institute of Arthritis
9650 Rockville Pike
Bethesda, MD 20814
Phone # 1-301-571-8314
(or) Phone # 1-301-496-8190
TTY # 1-301-565-2966
FAX # 1-301-571-0619
E-Mail: exec@anatomy.org

National Institute of Health
Bethesda, MD 20892
Phone # 1-301-496-4000
E-Mail: NIHInfo@OD.NIH.GOV
Internet: http://www.nih.gov/health/infoline.htm

National Institute of Osteoporosis
1232 22nd Street, N.W.
Washington, DC 20037
Phone # 1-800-624-2663
(or) Phone # 1-202-223-0344
TTY # 1-202-466-4315
Internet: www.osteo.org

National Women's Health Information Center
8550 Arlington Blvd., Suite 300
Fairfax, VA 22031

Phone # 1-800-994-WOMAN
TTY # 1-888-220-5446
Internet: www.4woman.gov

National Women's Health Network
514 10th Street N.W., Suite 400
Washington, DC 20004
Phone # 1-202-347-1140
FAX # 1-202-347-1168

National Women's Health Resource Center
2440 M Street, NW, Suite 201
Washington, DC 20037

Nature Made
P.O. Box 9606
Mission Hills, CA 91346
Phone # 1-800-276-2878
FAX # 1-818-221-6600
* Ask a Wellness Advisor Expert on the Internet at:
http://www.naturemade.com

New York Memory and Health Aging Services
65, East 76th Street
New York, NY 10021
E-Mail: info@nymemory.org

North American Menopause Society
University Hospitals Dept. of OB/GYN
2074 Abington Road
Cleveland, OH 44106
Phone # 1-800-774-5342
(or) Phone # 1-440-442-7550
FAX # 1-216-844-3348
E-Mail: www.menopause.org

One-a-Day
Bayer Corporation

36 Columbia Road
P.O. Box 1910
Morristown, NJ 07962
Phone # 1-800-331-4536
Phone # for One-a-Day Herbals # 1-800-800-4793
Internet: www.BayerCare.com

Soybean Association
12125 Woodcrest Executive Dr., Suite 100
St. Louis, MO 63141
Phone # 1-314-576-1770

Soyfoods Association of America
1723 U. Street, NW
Washington, DC 20009
Phone # 1-202-986-5600

Soy Protein Council
1255 23rd Street. NW, Suite 200
Washington, DC 20037
Phone # 1-202-467-6610

Speaking of Women's Health Foundation
1223 Central Parkway
Cincinnati, Ohio 45214
Phone # 1-866-SWH-INFO
Internet: www.speakingofwomenshealth.com

Susan G. Komen Foundation
Phone # 1-800- I M AWARE (or) Phone # 1-800-462-9273
Internet: www.komen.org

United Soybean Board
424 2nd Avenue West
Seattle, WA 98119
Phone # 1-206-270-4641
Internet: www.talksoy.com

Web MD
* Ask an Expert on-line at:
E-Mail: http://www.webmd.com

Women's Health Resource Center
1342 Taubman Center
University of Michigan Health System
Ann Arbor, MI 48109
Phone # 1-734-647-0448
(or) Phone # 1-734-936-8886
FAX # 1-734-936-5473
Internet: www.med.umich.edu/whp

World Health Organization
Internet: http://www.who.int
E-Mail: hoganm@who.ch

Dictionary Plus for WOMEN

Bibliography

Suzette Buhr. **36 Going On 50.** 1998-99. Real Life Experience Of Hysterectomy & Menopause.

Christiane Northrup, M.D. OB/GYN. **American Health For Women**. October 1998. Page 18; All Natural Hot Flash Helpers.

Ellen Michand, Elisabeth Torg, Editors Of Prevention Magazine Health Books. **Total Health For Women**. 1995. Definitions Of Words, Endometriosis And Hysterectomy.

American Academy Of Family Physicians And Lydia T. Dorsky, And Robert Dorsky, D.M.D.. **Family Circle**. April 1999. Healthy Living; Living Well After Menopause.

Krames Communication. **Hysterectomy**. 1998. When Surgery Is The Solution.

Krames Communication. **Menopause.** 1996. Your Guide To Feeling Good In A New Stage Of Life.

Wyeth-Ayerst Laboratories (Pharmaceutical Co.). **Discover More About Menopause And E.R.T**. 1998. E.R.T. For Hysterectomized Women.

The American College Of Obstetricians And Gynecologists. **Women's Health**. 1997, 1998. Pamphlets: Preventing Osteoporosis, The Menopause Years, Hormone Replacement Therapy, And Laparoscopy.

Greg Sushinsky. **Herbs That Heal And Cure**. 1998. Herbs And Their Uses.

Anne McIntyre. **The Medicinal Garden**. 1997. Herbs And Their Ailments.

David Kessler, M.D. with Sheila Buff. **The Doctors Complete Guide To Healing Herbs.** 1996. Herbal Remedies For Lifelong Good Health.

Deborah R. Mitchell. **Dictionary Of Natural Healing.** 1998. Herbs, Ailments And Their Possible Treatments.

One-A-Day And Dr. Judith Stern, Ph.D.. **The Right Combination.** 1999. Herbs, Health And You.

Dictionary Plus for WOMEN

Newsweek. **Health For Life, Special Edition.** Spring/Summer 1999. What Every Woman Needs To Know.

Family Circle. **Your Family's Health.** Spring 1999. Cancer, Heart, Womens Issues, And Headaches.

Shari Lieberman, PhD And Nancy Bruning. **The Real Vitamin & Mineral Book.** 1997. Second Edition; Guide To Nutritional Supplements.

American Cancer Society. **Cancer Facts & Figures.** 2002. Cancer Statistics.

National Institutes Of Health. **Cancer Of The Uterus, Cancer Of The Cervix, & Ovarian Cancer.** 1988, 1990, & 1993. What You Need To Know About (Info Booklets).

John M. Ellis, M.D. And Jean Pamplin. **Vitamin B 6 Therapy.** 1999. Nature's Versatile Healer.

On-line Info: **http://www.solgar.com/nutrition_library/vitamin guide.html** Guide To Vitamins And Minerals—Solgar Vitamin And Herb Company. 2002

On-line Info: **http://www.inx.net/~health/vitamins.html** Morgan Health Vitamin Reference Guide. 2002

On-line Info: **http://www.allocca.com/ch_9.html** Clinical Nutrition For The Balanced Body, 2nd Edition. 2002

On-line Info: **http://www.room42.com/store/health_nutrition/vitamins_minerals.html** Vitamins And Minerals. Center For All Your Health, Mind, & Body Int. 2002

Gerard J. Tortora and Nicholas P. Anagnostakos. **Principles Of Anatomy And Physiology.** 1990. 6th Edition. HarperCollins Publishers.

On-line Info: **http://www.ultrapms.com/pms/index.html**. PMS Info, Vitamin & Mineral Info. 2002.

On-line Info: **http://home.coqui.net/ytorres/NHRT/art, 11.htm** "Natural" vs. "Synthetic" Hormones, A question of Semantics. John R. Lee, MD. 2002

On-line Info: **http://www.progestnet.com/documents/synthetic.html** What is Progesterone? Synthetic Progestins are not the same as Natural Progesterone. Progesterone Advocates Network. 2002

On-line Info: **http://www.wcmh.org/healthinformation/Women's%20 Health%20Guide/6383.htm** Fibroids, Endometriosis, and Menopause Info. 2002

On-line Info: **http://members.tripod.com/~NCR/osteofacts.html** Osteoporosis. 2002

On-line Info: **http://www.findarticles.com** Gale Encyclopedia of Medicine. Anesthesia Information. 2002

Taber's Cyclopedic Medical Dictionary. 1981. By: F.A. Davis Company. Medical Definitions/Information.

On-line Info: **http://www/besthealth.com/library/lapdiag.html** Laparoscopy and Uterus Information. 2002

On-line Info: **http:www.med.umich.edu/1libr/crs/abhys.htm** University of Michigan Health System. 2002

On-line Info: **http://www.folsomobgyn.com/hysterectomy,_vaginal.htm** Vaginal Hysterectomy Information. 2002

On-line Info: **http://www.premarin.com/ForWomen/1070.asp** Moving through Menopause. 2002

Remedy Publication. "A Time Of Change", page 36. Fall 2001.

On-line Info: **http://www.fwhc.org/menomyth22.htm** Feminist Women's Health Center. Menopause: Myths vs. Facts. Vitamin Information. 2002

On-line Info: **http://www.naturalvitality.net/pages/facts.htm** Menopausitive; Natural Daily Support for Menopause. Menopause Facts. 2002

On-line Info: **http://www.mayoclinic.com** A variety of Medical Information. 2002

On-line Info. **http://www.webmd.com.** A variety of Medical Information. 2002

On-line Info: **http://www.soyfoods.com/nutrition/isoflavoneconcentration.html** U.S. Soyfoods Directory; Soy and Isoflavone Information. 2002

On-line Info: **http://www.soy.com/Soy_Information/Reference/Isoflavonesgeneral.html** Soycorn; Soy and Isoflavone Information. 2002

On-line Info: **http://www.pslgroup.com/dg/5b68e.htm** Webmaster@docguide.com Doctor's Guide, Global Edition Dry Mouth in Sjogren's Syndrome. 1995

On-line Info: **http://ada.org/public/topics/drymouth.html** The American Dental Asociation, Topic: Dry Mouth. 2002

On-line Info: **http://dentistry.about.com/library/weekly/aa051498.htm** Dentistry; Xerostomia (Dry Mouth). May 1998

On-line Info: **http://www.youreyesite.corn/menopause.htm** Shady Grove Eye and Vision Care. Source—JAMA 2001

On-line Info: **http://www.pslgroup.com/dq/8372.htm** Webmaster@docguide.com Doctor's Guide; Global Edition Eye Care for Pregnant and Menopausal Women. 1995

On-line Info: **http://www.contactlensinstitute.com/mo1199.htm** Contact lens Institute/Optometry. Dry Eye Syndrome. 1997

On-line Info: **http://www.stlukeseye.com/Conditions/DryEyeSyndrome.asp** St. Luke's Clinic. Dry Eye Syndrome information. 2001

On-line Info: **http://www.visionworksusa.com/faq.asp** Dry Eye Syndrome. 2002

On-line Info: **http://health.discovery.com/diseasesandcond/encyclopedia/813.html** Discovery Health Channel. Surgery. Health Answers. 2001

On-line Info: **http://www.infoplease.com/ce6/sci/A0839601.html** Learning Network; Infoplease.com. Polyp. 2002

On-line Info: **http://www.ethiconinc.com/facts/women/fibroids/body.htm** GYNECARE. Fibroids and Polyps. 2000

The American College of Obstetricians and Gynecologists. **Understanding Hysterectomy. Hysteroscopy. Uterine Fibroids. Dilation and Curettage. The Pap Test. Important Facts about Endometriosis. Disorders of the Cervix.** Patient Educational Materials. 1998 and 1999.

Dictionary Plus for WOMEN

Genevieve Love Smith and Phyllis E. Davis. **Medical Terminology; 4th Edition.** A Wiley Medical Publication. 1981

On-line Info: **http://www.hcrc.org/faqs/calcium.html** Health Care Reality Check. Calcium Supplements. By: Maida Taylor, MD, MPH, FACOG. 2002

On-line Info: **http://www.healthy.net/asp/templates/article.asp? Page Type=article&ID=1379** Phenomena; Natural Health and Beauty Technology. Fibrocystic Breast Disease. By: Susan M. Lark, M.D. 2002

On-line Info: **http://www.health-alliance.com/contentarchive/october00/women.html** Healthy Alliance/Healthy Living. Fibrocystic Breast Disease. October 2000

On-line Info: **http://my.webmd.com/content/asset/miller_keane_ 12744** Web MD Health. Fibrocystic Disease of the Breast. Miller-Keane Medical Dictionary. 2000

On-line Info: **http://my.webmd.com/content/article/1662.52439** Web MD Health. Types of Benign Breast Lumps. The Cleveland Clinic. 2002

On-line Info: **http://www.findarticles.com/cf_dls/g2603/0003/2603000364/pl/article.jhtml** Find Articles. The Gale Encyclopedia of Alternative Medicine. 2002

On-line Info: **www.findarticles.com** Topic: Memory Loss. 2002

On-line Info: **http://www.nymemory.org/appointments.html** The New York Memory and Healthy Aging Services. ABC's of Aging, Alzheimer's, Estrogen & Memory. Appointments and Evaluations. 2002

On-line Info: **http://www.nymemory.org/menmemandmoo.html** The New York Memory and Healthy Aging Services. ABC's of Aging, Alzheimer's, Estrogen, & Memory. Women and Alzheimer's Disease. 2002

American Cancer Society. **Cancer Facts For Women.** Patient Educational Material. 2001

On-line Info: **http://www.Fibrocystic.com/** Fibrocystic Breast Disease. 2002

On-line Info: **http://www.hotflash.org/dismen.shtml** Women's Health Issues. Hotflashes. R.K. West Consulting. 2002

On-line Info: **http://aolsvc.health.webmd.aol.com** Web MD with AOL Health. Your Guide to Menstrual Cramps. The Cleveland Clinic. 2002

On-line Info. **http://www.premarin.com/ForWomen/1070.asp** (and) **http://www.premarin.com/default.asp** Premarin. Moving through Menopause. 2002

On-line: **http://www.aomc.org/abysurg.html** Exercise & Mobility. 2002

Ethicon Endo-Surgery, Inc. A Johnson & Johnson Company. **A Woman's Guide to Mammotome, The Easier Biopsy.** Educational Information Video. 2002

On-line Info: **http://aolsvc.illnesses.aol.com/DS00328/main.html** Mayo Clinic Health Information. What is Breast Cancer? Mayo Foundation for Medical Education and Research. 2001

On-line Info: **http://www.findarticles.com** The Gale Encyclopedia of Medicine. Dysfunctional Uterine Bleeding. 1999

On-line Info: **http://intl-theoncologist.alphamedpress.org/cgi/content/full/5/5/388** The Oncologist. Raloxifene information. By: Douglas B. Muchmore. 2000

On-line Info: **http://www.oncli.net/raloxifene** Oncology Care. Ask an Oncologist about Raloxifene. Webmaster@oncli.com. 2002

On-line Info: **http://www.progestnet.com/documents/hormone_level_ testing.html** Progesterone Advocates Network. Hormone Level Testing. 1999

On-line Info: **http://www.druginfonet.com/faq/new/DISEASE_FAQ/Osteoporosis.htm** Infolink, The internet source for healthcare information. Doctors' Answers to "Frequently Asked Questions"— Osteoporosis. Drug Info Net. 1997

On-line Info: **http://www.findarticles.com** Gale Encyclopedia of Medicine: Anesthesia, general. 1999

On-line Info: **http://www.howstuffworks.com/anesthesial.htm** Marshall Brain's How Stuff Works. "How Anesthesia Works". 2002

On-line Info: **http://www.wcmh.org/healthinformation/Women's %20health%20Guide/6383.htm** Uterine Fibroids, **18314.htm** Treating Endometriosis, **6386.htm** Endometriosis. 2002

On-line Info. **http://www.naturalvitality.net/pages/facts.htm** Menopausitive; Natural Daily Support for Menopause. Menopause Facts. 2002

On-line Info: **http://www.mayoclinic.corn/invoke.cfm?id=HQ01634** Complementary and Alternative Medicine. Glucosamine for Arthritis. 2002

On-line Info: **http://www.dmc.org/health_info/topics/wome3275.html** Prolapsed Bladder or Rectum. 2001

On-line Info: **http://www.med.umich.edu/1libr/crs/abhys.htm** University of Michigan Health System. Patient Advisor. Uterus Removal, Abdominal (Hysterectomy). 2002

On-line Info: **http://www.folsomobgyn.com/hysterectomy,_vaginal.htm** Vaginal Hysterectomy. 2002

On-line Info: **http://www.breastcancerinfo.com/bhealth/html/ tamoxifen.asp** Komen: Tamoxifen as a Treatment for Breast Cancer. 2002

On-line Info: **http://www.oncli.net/tamoxifen/** Oncology Care. Ask an Oncologist about Tamoxifen. Webmaster@oncli.com. 2002

On-line Info: **http://www.ultrapms.com/pms/index.shtml** PMS, Vitamin, and Mineral Info. 2002

On-line Info: **http://www.fwhc.org/menomyth22.htm** Feminist Women's Health Center. Menopause: Myths vs. Facts. 2000

Bayer. **Get Smart about Cardiovascular Disease.** 2002. Heart Health Information For Women.

Speaking of Women's Health. **Preventing and Treating Osteoporosis. Living With Arthritis. Alternative & Complementary Medicine. Living With Menopause. Heart Disease. Memory. Better Nutrition For Life. Oral Health. Skin Care. Hysterectomy. PMS. Breast Cancer. Urinary Tract Infections. Sleep.** Wal-Mart Stores, Inc. 2002

Stephen Holt, M.D.. **The Soy Revolution.** 1998. Dell Publishing.

On-line Info: **http://www.hcrc.org/contrib/coleman/herbs.html** Herbs For Health; By Ellen Cloeman, RD, MA, MPH. 2002

Dictionary Plus for WOMEN

On-line Info: **http://www.holisticonline.com/Herbal-Med/_Herbs /h211.htm** Herb Information; Vitex. 2000

On-line Info: **http://www.herbs.org/current/vitexpms.html** Herb World News Online—Research Reviews. Vitex Information. 2000

On-line Info: **http://www.kava-alert.com/** Kava Information. 2002

On-line Info: **http://www.kickbackwithkava.com/** Kava Kava Information. 2002

On-line Info: **http://www.kcweb.com/herb/echin.htm** Herbal Information Center; Echinacea. **kavakava.htm** Herbal Information Center; Kava Kava **hawthorn.htm** Herbal Information Center: Hawthorn 2002

On-line Info: **http://fatimahtaher.tripod.com/intro.htm** Ginko Biloba Information. 2002

On-line Info: **http://www.valleyherbs.com/ginko.html** Health Line; By Brent Hauver. Memory Enhancer and Brain Food Ginko Biloba. 2002

On-line Info: **http://www.findarticles.com** Gale Encyclopedia of Alternative Medicine: dongquai. 2001

On-line Info: **http://www.askapot.com/prod_info/black_cohosh.htm** Black Cohosh for Relief of Menstruation Symptoms. 2002

On-line Info: **http://families-first.com/hotflash/faq/black-cohosh.htm** Hotflash!—FAQ—Black Cohosh. 2002

On-line Info: **http://www.health-pages.com/bc/** Whole Health. Black Cohosh. 2002

On-line Info: **http://www.naturemade.com/ProductDatabase/** Nature Made Information: St. John's Wort, Vinpocetine, Ginseng, Soy, Garlic, Ginko Biloba, and Echinacea. 2002

On-line Info: **http://www.yellowapple.com a_kavakava.htm** Kava Plus **a_ginko_biloba.htm** Ginko Plus **a_stjohnswort.htm** St. John's Wort Plus Yellowapple.com; Natural Health Products. 2000

University of Wisconsin, Madison. **Radiology Notes, Anatomy and Physiology Notes.** By: Suzette Buhr. 1983-1985.

Wynn Kapit / Lawrence M. Elson. **The Anatomy Coloring Book.** 1977. Harper & Row, Publishers, Inc.

Phillip W. Ballinger. **Merrill's Atlas of Radiographic Positions and Radiographic Procedures.** 1982. 5th Edition.

Royce L. Montgomery, Ph.D. **Basic Anatomy for the Allied Health Professions.** 1980. Urban & Schwarzenberg.

On-line Info: **http.//home.inreach.com/trilight/maca_root.htm** Maca Root Information. 2002

On-line Info: **www.nutraceutic.com/Products/AmazonHerbs/maca.htm** Maca—Peruvian Ginseng Information. 2002

On-line Info: **http://all-about-menopause.com/making_sense _of_menopause.htm** Making Sense of Menopause. Medicine-Plants.com. 2002

Lauri McKean. Information Lecture: **Tia Chi for Health and Well Being.** 2002. What is Tai Chi, and Basic Tai Chi Principles.

On-line Info: **http://www.personalhealthzone.com** Side Effects and Warnings for the following: Black Cohosh, Dong Quai, Echinacea, Garlic, Ginko Biloba, Ginseng, Hawthorn, Sarsaparilla, and St. John's Wort. 2002

On-line: **http://www.rxlist.com/cgi/alt/wildyam_faq.htm** Wild Yam Information. 1999

On-line: **http://www.users.bigpond.com/wpm/** Wild Yam Information. By. Life Extension Associates. 2002

On-line Info: **http://www.onedietstore.com/wild_yam.htm** Nature's Sunshine: Wild Yam Information. 2002

Meriter Hospital (Madison, Wisconsin). **Complementary Medicine.** Accent on Health, classes. 2002. Alternative Medicine Choices.

Winnifred B. Cutler, Ph.D. **Hysterectomy: Before & After.** A Comprehensive Guide to Preventing, Preparing For, and Maximizing Health After Hysterectomy. 1988. HarperPerennial Publishers.

University of Michigan Health System. **Understanding Pelvic Floor Disorders.** 2002. Women's Health Resource Center. (www.med.umich.edu/whp)

On-line Info: **http://aolsvc.health.webmd.aol.com** Web MD with AOL Health. Toxic Shock Syndrome. 2001

On-line: **http://www.aabhealth.corn/soy.htm** Background on Soy. The Advantages of Soy. By: SoyBiotics. 2002

On-line Info: **http://vegweb.com/articles/38.shtml** The Healing Power of Soy's Isoflavones. By: Monique N. Gilbert, B.Sc. 2002

On-line Info: **http://www.acog.org** ACOG News Release. Daily Soy Reduces Hot Flashes and Lowers Cholesterol. 2002

WEA Trust. **Taking Care: Health Information You Can Count On.** April 2002. Get Heart-Healthy With Soy.

Herbalife International, Inc.. **A Way of Life.** 2001. Live Better Through Herbal Nutrition.

Wisconsin State Journal. **Use of Male Sex Hormone is Growing.** By: Patricia Simms. July 28, 2002.

Wisconsin State Journal. **Many Doctors, Scientists Skeptical of Saliva Tests.** By: Patricia Simms and Deborah Kades. June 24, 2002.

Wisconsin State Journal. **Debate Rages Over Designer Hormones.** By: Patricia Simms and Deborah Kades. June 23, 2002.

Sandra Cabot, MD. **Smart Medicine for Menopause.** 1995. Avery Publishing Group, Inc.

Public Service Message by: MGI Pharma, Inc. **"What's Happening To Me?"** Re: Sjogren's Syndrome. Arthritis Today Magazine. July—August 2002.

On-line Info: **http://www.nih.gov/icd** National Institute of Health. History Information. 2002

On-line Info: **http://www.herbal-concepts.co.uk/history.html** Herbal History Information. 2002

Women's Health America. **Natural Hormone Replacement: What You Need To Know.** 2002

Dictionary Plus for WOMEN

On-line Info: **http://youngagain.com** Hormone Information. 2002

On-line Info: **http://www.bfe.org** Pelvic Floor Disorder Information. 2002

On-line Info: **www.medhelpinternational** Adrenal Gland Information. 1996

On-line Info: **www.EndocrineWeb.com** Your Adrenal Glands. 1997, 1998

On-line Info: **http://www.obgyn.net** Menopause, Perimenopause, & Postmenopause: Definitions, Terms & Concepts. By: Peter Kenemans, MD, PhD. 2002

On-line Info: **http://www.menopause.org/news.html** Menopause Information. 2002

On-line Info: **http://www.arbonnconsultantonline.com/Perimenopause_and_You.htm** Perimenopause and You. 2002

On-line Info: **http://www.fibrocystic.com** Fibrocystic Breast Disease. 2002

On-line Info: **http://www.obgyn.net** Pelvic Floor Disorders. 2000

On-line Info: **http://www.drbob4health.com** Estrogen Replacement Therapy. 2002

On-line Info: **http://inventors.about.com/library/inventors/** The History of Breakfast Cereals. 2002

On-line Info: **http://isd.ingham.kl2.mi.us/~mich/indust.html** John Harvey Kellogg. 2002

On-line Info: **www.cancer.gov** Postmenopausal Hormone Use. 7-16-2002

On-line Info: **http://www.ama-assn.org** American Medical Association. 2002

On-line Info: **http://www.healthhelper.com** History of Herbal Medicine. 2002

On-line Info: **www.Evista.com** Raloxifene Information. 2001

On-line Info: **http://www.optimalnp.com/natural_hormones.htm** The Natural (bio-identical) human hormones consist of... 2002

On-line Info: **http://www.towntotal.corn/hormone.html** Natural Hormone Replacement. 2002

Turville Bay MRI Centers. **MRI Patient Information Pamphlet.** 2002. Madison, Wisconsin.

Dean Foundation. **Bone Densitometry, Patient Information.** 2002. Madison, Wisconsin.

Wisconsin State Journal. **Common Sense Will Overcome Lack of HRT.** By: Susan Ager. July 21, 2002.

On-line Info: **http://www.who.int/home-page/** World Health Organization Information. 2002

On-line Info: **www.iahf.com** International Advocates for Health Freedom. 2002

Women's Health Resource Center. **Understanding Pelvic Floor Disorders.** 2002. University of Michigan Health System.

On-line Info: **http://web.iquest.net/ofma/fda.htm** Food & Drug Administration Information. 2002

On-line Info: **http.//store.yahoo.com/healingherbsofchina/10myths.html** 10 Myths About Herbs & Healing. 2002

On-line Info: **http://ilhwa-nz.virtualave.net/**Ginseng Information. 2002

University of Michigan Health System. **Women and Weight.** Summer 2002. Women's Health Information.

American Cancer Society. **Cancer Prevention & Early Detection.** 2002. Cancer Facts & Figures.

Remedy Publication. "A Skin Cancer Glossary", page 40. Spring 2002.

On-line Info: **www.askjeeves.com** Ask Questions. 2002

On-line Info: **www.plannedparenthood.org/WOMENSHEALTH/menopause.htm** Menopause—Another Change in Life. 2002

On-line Info: **www.fda.com** U.S. Food & Drug Administration Regulations. 2002

On-line Info: **http://www.antiaging-systems.net** International Antiaging Systems. Menopause Information. 2002

On-line Info: **http://abcnews.go.com** Good Morning America. (Ginko Health Info.) A Memorable Herb? August 21, 2002

Journal of the American Medical Association. **Ginko For Memory Enhancement.** August 21, 2002. JAMA

Newsweek. **Letters to the Editor.** August 5, 2002. Rethinking Hormone Therapy.

Newsweek. **And Now For A Hot Flash.** July 29, 2002. The Last Word, By: Anna Quindlen.

Newsweek. **The End Of The Age Of Estrogen.** July 22, 2002. By: Geoffrey Cowley and Karen Springen.

Time. **The Truth About Hormones.** July 22, 2002. By: Christine Gorman and Alice Park.

National Institute on Aging. **Menopause: One Woman's Story, Every Woman's Story/A Resource for Making Healthy Choices.** February 2001. Menopause Information.

FlexAble. **FlexAble Joint Care Supplements.** 2002. Frequently Asked Questions. (www.flexablebrand.com)

Wisconsin State Journal. **Dietary Supplements: Proceed With Caution.** September 1, 2002.

On-line Info: **http://www.fda.gov/cder/handbook/index.htm** (or) **http://www.cfsan.fda.gov/~dms/supplmnt.html** Food and Drug Administration Information. 2002

On-line Info: **http://healthlink.mcw.edu/article/997669927.html** Health Link. Coping with Discomfort of Mammograms. 2002

On-line Info: **http://www.medexpert.net/medinfo/mammogra.htm** MedExpert.net. Mammography and Breast Imaging. 2002

On-line Info: **http://www.wholefoods.com/healthinfo/polysorbate80.html** Whole Foods Market. Ingredients: Polysorbate 80. 2002

Dictionary Plus for WOMEN

On-line Info: **www.NatureMade.com** Ask and Expert On-line. Re: Food & Nutrition. 2002

On-line Info: **http://www.washingtonpost.com** FDA to Weigh New Controls on Problematic Drugs. By: Francesca Lunzer Kritz. The Washington Post. April 16, 2002.

About the Author

Suzette Buhr lives in Wisconsin with her husband, Jim and their two children, Alicia and Josh. It was during her own personal experience of going through a hysterectomy and menopause, at the age of 36, that she began her research on these subjects.

Her educational background includes: graduating from Sun Prairie High School 1980, graduating from University of Wisconsin—Madison as a Registered Technologist in Radiology 1985, and completing 1 year of American Sign Language at Madison Area Technical College 2000. Suzette's medical employment history has included: U.W. Hospital and Clinics (Northeast Family Practice), Dean Medical Center, Dr. Wanek's Orthodontic Office, and Dental Health Associates.

She enjoys her creative writing skills & photography and has been published in a variety of magazines, books, and newspapers including: Country Extra, Birds and Blooms, Country Discoveries, This Old Barn, The Good Land, Taste of Home, Photographer's Edge, Working Mother Magazine, Cleo/Gibson Greeting Card Company, The Wisconsin State Journal/Capital Times, Common Sense, Wisconsin Trails, Travel America, and Wisconsin Department of Tourism Guide Books.

Suzette is currently working on other topics that will comprise the series for her Dictionary Plus books. To see a complete listing, visit online at www.1stbooks.com

More Dictionary Plus Titles

Dictionary Plus for Men
An information guidebook regarding: Male Menopause, Prostate Health, and Related Topics.

Dictionary Plus for Your Dental and Orthodontic Health
An information guidebook regarding: The Care and Maintenance of Teeth and the Oral Surroundings.

Dictionary Plus for Teenagers and Parents of Teenagers
An information guidebook regarding: Teenage Topics.

Dictionary Plus for Your Allergies, Asthma, Sinus, Ears, Nose, & Throat
An information guidebook regarding: Every Breath We Take and How It Affects Us.

Dictionary Plus for Seniors and the Caretakers of Seniors
An information guidebook regarding: Aging and Caring For the Elderly.

Dictionary Plus for the Fears Inside of Us
An information guidebook regarding: Phobias, Fears, and Hypochondriacs.

Dictionary Plus for Dreamers
An information guidebook regarding: Dreams, Preminitions, and the Psychic Ability that Everyone Has.

Printed in the United States
124294LV00001B/5/A